A MAN FOR MRS. CLAUS

REBEKAH WEATHERSPOON

BOOKS BY REBEKAH

PHASE ONE

FIT & CO.

Fit

Tamed

Sated

Wrapped

LOOSE ENDS

Rafe: A Buff Male Nanny

Xeni: A Marriage of Inconvenience

Meegan: A Holidate for Hire

COWBOYS OF CALIFORNIA

A Cowboy To Remember

If The Boot Fits

A Thorn In The Saddle

BEARDS & BONDAGE

Haven

Sanctuary

Harbor

SUGAR BABY NOVELLAS

So Sweet

So Right

So For Real

VAMPIRE SORORITY SISTERS

Better Off Red

Blacker Than Blue

Soul To Keep

STAND ALONE TITLES

The Fling

At Her Feet

Treasure

A Walk In the Park

YOUNG ADULT

Her Good Side

PHASE TWO

A Man For Mrs. Claus

ABOUT THIS BOOK

Running the North Pole and making good on the promise of comfort and joy for a few billion people is no simple two-step around the Christmas tree. Mr. and Mrs. Claus have always worked in tandem to do just that. So when her third husband realizes it's time to peace out and move on to more Heavenly pastures, the angels and all the elves know what time it is. They need to find Tiffany Saint-Nicholas a new man.

With the holiday calendar slowing down for no one, her team has three days to find her a new Santa. Someone kind, loving and willing to take on the spirit of the season, and with the potential to be Tiffany's *first* true love match. Tiffany thinks that idea is cute and all, and so are the men they line up for her. But she knows delivering on their Christmas obligations is what really matters, not the chemistry she might have with the candidates in question. Too bad one prospective Santa will stop at nothing to show her and the rest of the North Pole population that no amount of silver or gold is more important than winning Tiffany's heart.

For my dad.
Thanks for answering all of my questions about firetrucks
and sitting through one whole episode of 9-1-1.

1

Tiffany Saint-Nicholas closed her eyes against the slowly building earthquake on the other side of her bed. Even though it had been decades since she'd felt the sensation so close, that didn't change its meaning. She hoped the rumbling would stop. Maybe they had made a mistake? But, after a few long moments, the shaking humming only grew stronger. Carefully, Tiffany slid out of bed, refusing to look in Laurence's direction. She stepped into her Garfield slippers, then grabbed her red robe off its gilded hook on the far wall.

Button, the Saint Bernard, perched his front paws on the foot of the bed, watching the light show coming from her soon-to-be ex-husband. The other dogs, Argos and Shadow, couldn't be bothered. They knew the drill. Argos snoozed on the plush rug, while Shadow followed her to the bathroom. Tiffany let out another sigh as she looked at herself in the mirror. By human standards, she looked great for two hundred and thirty-one years old. Still, frustration and something close to pain settled in her chest, making her feel a thousand years older.

She knew what she'd signed up for, what she'd agreed to, and she knew that all she had to do was say the word and she could move on. Moving on wasn't what she wanted, though, and everyone—*they*—knew that. Too bad her singular, silly desires didn't change the way the system worked. As if to drive the point home, she watched as her hair, still up in its rollers, bled from a rich white back to its original shiny, jet black. Tiffany closed her eyes, gave her head a good shake and the rollers themselves disappeared.

She shook her head one more time, focusing on a style she'd seen about thirty years ago that didn't fit the vibe of her job or her marriage. She could have waited until after she talked to her team and the children, but she didn't see the point. She leaned closer to the mirror, examining the blowout bob. After she tucked one side behind her delicately pointed ears, the look seemed to really come together.

"What do you think, girl?" she asked Shadow, keeping her voice low. Tiffany glanced over as the black lab looked back, giving her a silent nod of doggy approval. "I think so too. Well, let's go say goodbye."

As she expected, Laurence was out of bed, standing in front of the window in his boxers, looking out at the village like he did every morning. This time though, his whole body was aglow as black, white, silver and gold sparkling orbs seemed to light him from the inside. Even from the back she could tell he looked younger. His white locs, which usually fell mid-back, were gone and so was his white beard. In their place were the tight, black afro and the clean-shaven cheeks he'd had when they first met. When he turned to her and she saw the whites of his eyes replaced with prisms, she knew he'd gotten the news he'd been secretly waiting for this whole time.

A warm smile spread across Tiffany's face. She crossed the room, reached through the warm, glittering illumination that surrounded him and took his hand. "Leaving so soon?" She couldn't resist the urge to tease him one last time.

Laurence chuckled and gave her hand a little squeeze. The joy was practically leaping off him. "Dottie had her home-going this morning. She's finally at rest."

"And she asked for you." Laurence nodded.

"Well, we can't send you up there in your draws." Tiffany stepped back a bit and snapped her fingers. In a flash, Laurence was back in his yellow-collared shirt, brown sweater, denim Lee Riders and tan shoes, same as the first day she met him. "That's much better."

"I like the hair. It suits you." He reached out and lightly touched one of her soft waves.

"I won't have some weirdo in my bed anymore, telling me how much he liked it long," she groaned playfully, rolling her eyes.

"What can I say? You look good with those long white curls. I'll miss them."

"No, you won't," she replied, her smile genuine. "You won't even think about me. And that's how it's supposed to be."

"Thank you. For everything, Tiff. I mean it."

Tiffany waved him off. "The pleasure was all mine. Did you say goodbye to the children?"

"I did. I left the Spirit with Waltie."

"Of course you did."

Laurence let out his signature belly laugh before crouching down on one knee. The dogs didn't hesitate. They trotted right to him and Tiffany almost broke, watching him ruffle their fur and baby talk to them one last time. For a moment, she thought he might use them to stall a little longer. They'd only appeared for him in the first place, but Laurence gave them each a quick kiss on the head and then turned to face her.

"I should go."

Tiffany nodded, swallowing the lump in her throat. She stepped closer and adjusted his collar. "Go get your girl."

"You'll find someone better, Tiff. I know it."

"Nah. No one's topping you. Never."

"Of course you will. You have excellent taste. Just look at the last champion who made the cut."

"Ha! That is true."

"It's only up from here." Laurence reached for her hand, brushing his lips across her knuckles, the warm glow around him growing stronger. And with a wink, he was gone.

Tiffany stood there longer than she wanted to, her eyes still processing the sparkling outline of the man she'd grown to love and deeply respect. He'd done the job so well, but she was glad that giving him her heart had never been an option. She would miss her friend so much and she would move on. She had to. It was her job. She'd go through the process and find a new partner who understood what they needed to do, how important the work was still. And this go-around, she wouldn't waste any time dreaming about a love of her own. Love was never on the table and never would be. Not for her. She had a job to do.

A soft doggy head brushing against her hand snapped her

out of her sullen trance. Tiffany had a long day ahead of her with a lot of meetings. She had to get with Shauna and restructure the calendar for as long as the selection process took—at least the next seventy-two hours. She had to spend a little extra time with the kids even though she knew they'd be fine. Laurence had left each one of them with the absolute knowledge that he loved them and always would, but she knew they needed to see that she was okay and ready to move on. She looked down at Button and gave him a firm scratch behind his ear.

"Come on, boy. It's time to find us a new Santa."

2

June seventeenth was a good day. A record heatwave had just passed through. Miss Lara, the cookie lady, stopped by the station house with double of everyone's favorites. The Lakers were forty-seven seconds from bringing home another O'Brien trophy. A situationship that was doomed from the start had come to a peaceful conclusion. It was the perfect day for Fire Engineer Dominick Bell to die. He stood in the kitchen, prepping some late night nachos fries for his crew, trying not to laugh at the scene playing out across the T.V. room.

"Come on, Colesmith. You bitch," Won-Lopez seethed.

"They're gonna win. Will you relax?" Howe laughed from the couch.

"He can't. He bet his truck on this title," Kiyohara blurted from the far end of the sectional.

"Man! Shut up!" Won-Lopez growled. Another time-out and commercial break. The Lakers were up by ten and there wasn't enough time on the clock for the Bucks to steal a win, but Won-Lopez was still sweating.

Fregosi stood from his seat, shaking his head. "Captain told your ass to stop betting on this shit. You should take his advice."

Won-Lopez just looked down at his phone screen, probably waiting for the text that would make or break his gambling career.

Dominick kept on chopping his onions. You'd think Won-Lopez would learn his lesson. He still owed from a Dodgers loss last week. He was an idiot, but he was also one of the best firefighters Station 94 had ever seen. Dominick wasn't lending him a dime, but he'd keep the details of Won-Lopez's stupid life choices a secret from the higher ups until someone came looking to break his kneecaps. After this game, on which he had bet nearly the value of his truck, Won-Lopez would be back to square, ready to live and gamble like a complete dummy another day.

It had been a typical shift. Two auto collisions with thankfully no major injuries and a small fire behind the 7-Eleven on La Cienega. A tree, some shrubs and a pile of garbage went up, and they were able to contain the flames before they spread to the store and small shopping plaza next door. Dominick had another twelve hours left of his tour and, while there was never a quiet day in the City of Los Angeles, he held out hope that they'd at least get through with no lives lost. He knew life and the job didn't always work that way, but he tossed up the same prayer at the beginning and end of every shift for good measure.

The ad for Instacart ended and the game resumed. Maxwell kicked the ball inbounds to Colesmith, who dropped behind the three-point line and drained a smooth bucket right before the buzzer rang.

"Thank fucking Christ," Won-Lopez gasped, grabbing his chest.

"What are you gonna do when you get in some real deep shit?" Howe laughed, standing from the couch, as the Lakers' bench cleared and confetti rained from the ceiling.

"Fake my death, steal your identity, flee to—" His destination was drowned out by the station alarm.

Dominick set down his knife, snapped off his prep gloves and followed Howe across the station house as they rushed to their gear. Moments later, Dominick was behind the wheel of engine 294, Howe in the Lieutenant's seat and Kiyohara in the third seat behind him, heading northwest on MLK Jr. Boulevard. Dominick couldn't have known it would be the last time they'd take this route. That he'd never see the headlights blaze across the sign for the Jackie Robinson stadium again. That it was the last time he'd have to wait for motorists to acknowledge the sirens on Obama and La Brea and get the fuck out of the way.

They cleared the intersection on Jefferson, where they could already see the telltale orange glow rising off to the West. And, though it was too dark to see now, Dominick would never contemplate pulling into the Popeyes on a sunny day as he spotted the Hollywood sign off in the distance. Traffic continued to part for their engines and the ambulance as they barreled down the avenue. He was glad he didn't flatten the kid on an electric scooter playing chicken with them as they turned left on Westhaven.

Three streets down, he and Howe could already see the reason for the call. Two sixty-foot palm trees were engulfed in flames. Dominick loved a Laker win as much as the next guy, but it was never reason for unsanctioned fireworks. He already knew what the homeowner would say, or the homeowner's teenage son who'd been left a butane torch and a box of sky hawk rockets. But, he wouldn't make it that far into the call.

Dominick had always loved to drive. It was the main reason he was behind the wheel of the rig. He'd never understood the appeal of street racing though, especially after he'd been to the scene of too many accidents caused by some young guys showing off. He'd never understand the logic, or even the physics, of getting a Honda Civic up to eighty miles an hour in a residential neighborhood with stop signs at every corner. He didn't have time to even turn his head to see the midnight blue coupe before it crashed right into the engineer's side door. Dominick wasn't ready for his life to end that night, on that call, but there was one silver lining. He was killed instantly and didn't feel a thing.

3

Dominick's lungs filled with the most soothing air. He exhaled and inhaled two more times before the sounds of a bouncing ball filled his ears. In and out three more times before he opened his eyes. His gaze cast down, he took in the sight of his hands resting on his thighs. He was still in his navy blue uniform tactical pants and his black work boots. He looked up as he pulled in another smooth breath. He knew where he was. Or, at least, the building looked familiar. He'd know the inside of the Staples Center anywhere. He'd never call it the Crypto Arena. Never. But, he'd never been court-side before and every other seat in the house was empty.

Three people were down at the left side of the court, all in emerald green track suits and crisp white sneakers. A white guy with really long blonde hair pulled back in a ponytail was in the middle of a playful game of one on one with a Black woman who had a crown of long locs twisted up in a bun on top of her head. The third person was a Black guy about

Dominick's age, leaning against the base of the hoop looking at a gold cellphone.

"You said best out of three," the woman laughed as she made a weak attempt to steal the ball.

"No." The white guy took a step back and tucked the ball under his arm. "I said first to three as many times as we can."

The Black guy glanced over at them and tucked his gold phone in his pocket. "It was best out of three. And you have one more game until we're out of here."

Dominick blinked, noticing something oddly pleasant about all three of their voices. Like church bells in the distance that you could still feel under your skin. He opened his mouth to ask what was happening and who they were when the Black guy looked over and smiled. The man started walking in his direction while the one-on-one game resumed under the net. Dominick still didn't know what the fuck was going on, but he stood anyway and started walking the other guy's way. They met close to half court and Dominick held out his hand. They shared a firm handshake.

"Dominick. How are you doing?"

"My man," the other guy said with another smile, this one wider and more brilliant up close. Whatever toothpaste he used was working. "I'm Gabriel. It's nice to meet you. Come on." He nodded toward the front row of empty chairs and guided Dominick back to the seat he'd just vacated with a gentle hand on his shoulder.

They both sat down, but Gabriel didn't say anything. Dominick knew why. He was supposed to ask something, but he couldn't wrap his mind around it at first, so he just watched the pick-up game play out in front of him. Finally he glanced over at Gabriel and tried to find his voice.

"I'm—I'm dead, aren't I?" At the three-point line, the Black woman stole the ball. She dribbled twice before a massive pair of gold wings unfurled from her back. Dominick could hear the air moving through each feather as she glided over the rim and dunked the ball. She flew up to the rafters, whooping over her victory. Dominick was again confused by the fact that he had absolutely no issue with what he saw. Of course angels can fly. Of course they like basketball. There was nothing weird happening here.

Gabriel let out an unnatural groan and crossed his leg, ankle propped up on his other knee. "Dominick, my friend, you are dead."

Dominick looked down, his mind suddenly searching for a how and a why, but all he could remember were the palm trees and his brain mentally running the procedure to get the engine in place near the hydrant.

"Just another foolish kid behind the wheel. He took out himself, his girlfriend who was riding shotgun, and you."

You assume a lot of danger when you go into a career like his, but this was not the way Dominick saw himself going out. And a basketball court was not the place he thought he'd end up. "Is this heaven?" he asked.

"No," Gabriel replied. "Think of this as more of a waiting room. Some people go straight up to paradise, like the girlfriend in question. She has one praying ass grandma. Tons of relatives waiting for her on the other side. Her boyfriend has to make a little pitstop and answer some questions before he moves on."

Dominick felt himself frown. He was a grown man now, with a good job and an inherent drive to always do what was right because, frankly, it caused you less problems in the long run. His sex life was amazing. His love life needed some work, but he was years and miles away from his time in foster care. There were no parents, no brothers and sisters he'd missed. Just one foster mom who he'd lost touch with and had since died. He'd been a real pain in her ass, so Dominick wasn't surprised she wasn't spending any time in the afterlife submitting prayers for him.

"Is that why I'm here? No one was waiting for me?"

"Nah. Mrs. Hobson is watching over you all the time and one person is more than enough where I'm from," Gabriel replied. "But that's not why I'm here."

"You need me to ref the next game?" Dominick said, confusing himself. He was dead. This wasn't a time for bad jokes. Or was it?

Gabriel let out a rich laugh. "No. It's something a little more important."

Suddenly at half court, a large door appeared. Dark oak with ornate carvings from top to bottom, with a white light around it. Even though it was yards away, Dominick could feel a gust of cold air coming from the sill.

"Now, you are dead," Gabriel went on. "There's nothing we can do about that. But you have two options."

"What are my options?"

"The first is that we can send you straight upstairs. A few people are waiting for you and a dog named Pinto?"

Dominick smiled, remembering his second foster dad's boxer. "He was a good dog."

"So there's Mrs. Hobson and Pinto, who'd like to say hello, or you could select door number one. We'd like you to interview for a job."

"What kind of job?"

"I can't tell you that. It's not my department, but I think it's a pretty good gig if you can get it." Gabriel nodded to the Black female angel whose wings were still on full display even though she was back on defense. "Jubilee put your name in the ring personally."

"Because I know what I'm talking about," she called back. "He'll be perfect."

Gabriel turned back to him, tilting his chin in the direction of the door. "What do you say?"

"There's nothing else you can tell me about it? Picking between a mystery door and Heaven seems like a bit of a gamble. What if this is the Bad Place and you're about to trick me into doing some demon's dirty work?"

"That was a good show, but no. We don't actually play those kinds of games. If you were going *down*, the intake process is a lot different and much more terrifying."

"Oh God, it smells so bad down there," Jubilee added.

Dominick looked back at the door, feeling a sudden undeniable pull. He couldn't explain it, just like he couldn't explain anything that was happening right now, but it was like a tug was coming from his gut and, more importantly, his heart. Even if he didn't get whatever job they were talking about, he had to see what was on the other side of that door.

"What happens if I don't get the job?"

"All good things. You can give me your faith with that, yeah?"

Dominick peered over at Gabriel. "Do you have wings too?"

Gabriel stood and backed up a couple feet, then his own set of golden wings unfurled from the shoulder seams of his tracksuit. Dominick let out another deep breath as the cool air from the door still brushed against his shins. He was definitely dead and that pull deep in his gut was still there. He stood and took a long, hard look at the door. While he was contemplating his future, if that even meant anything now, Jubilee flew over and landed like a graceful paraglider.

"Please say yes. Oliver wanted to pick a guy named Gary." She tilted her head back toward the White angel, who was practicing his free throw.

"Hey, Gary had potential!" Oliver shouted back.

"Gary had no potential," Jubilee whispered. "You got this. You're a good man, Dominick. You're exactly what she—"

Gabriel held up his hand, silencing her. Dominick looked between them, wondering who 'she' was, knowing that didn't change things. Gabriel already knew what his answer would be.

"Maybe I'll catch you guys later?" he said, swallowing the odd quiver in his voice.

Gabriel and Jubilee smiled brightly and nodded. Oliver, wings revealed, flew over and gave him a thumbs up of his own.

"Okay." Another deep breath and he moved toward the door. As he reached for the large iron knob in the middle of the heavy wood surface, Gabriel called out his name.

"Dominick?"

"Yeah?"

"Open your hand."

Dominick looked down. A medal of valor appeared in his open palm, the kind awarded by the City of Los Angeles. "What's this for?"

"Three years ago. The structure fire down on Exposition. They overlooked you."

Dominick felt the corner of his mustache pull up into a smile as he ran his thumb over the polished brass.

"That year, they gave it to this White guy from the 118 named Gary."

Dominick didn't know what the rules were when it came to making memories in the afterlife, but he was sure he would never forget the sound of angels laughing.

Not wasting another moment, he gripped the knob and gave it a solid push. Dominick soaked up the cool air that washed over him and then he stepped into the next phase of his existence.

4

As the bright light and cool air cleared, Dominick took in his new surroundings and then immediately froze in place. He hadn't known where he'd end up but he didn't expect to be standing in a hotel lobby. No one was at the reception desk, but Christmas music was piping through the overhead system. To his right, Dominick spotted a sign mounted on a metal stand.

Welcome to the North Pole Marriott Convention Center
Applicants This Way! ☞

Dominick ignored the decorative holly and sleigh bells around the text and arrow pointing down the corridor, and headed back to the double doors behind him. He stepped outside and took in the snowy landscape. Tall snow-covered pines and cascading mountains off in the distance were wrapped in what looked like train tracks. He'd been up to Big Bear and Tahoe, but this was nothing like that. Could he be in the real North Pole, whatever that meant? Maybe, but he wouldn't find out standing there in the cold. Dominick headed back inside and followed the signage.

The long hallway opened to a row of conference rooms. The one in the center had its door thrown open, more holly berries and garland draped around the door frame, and another **Welcome Applicants** sign inviting him in. Dominick wanted to be suspicious, because this whole thing was weird as hell. But, the feeling in his gut only grew stronger, warmer, propelling him forward step by step.

The conference room was small and definitely set up for an event. A few tables faced a wide screen at the front, with folders and red bags that looked like little Santa sacks at each seat. A few people milled around the room. A Black guy who looked a few years older than Dominick, clean shaved in green coveralls and a khaki hat with a city seal on it, was scoping out the long buffet table against the wall that was loaded down with a shit ton of food.

A tall, slim, Asian guy on the other side of the room was looking at the vintage holiday ads framed along the wall. A young white guy sat at one of the tables, looking down at something in his hand. Dominick noticed then that he didn't have his phone anymore. The only thing in his pocket was that Medal of Valor.

A short, heavy, brown guy was at the front of the room in one of the freshest navy blue suits Dominick had ever seen. His slick dark hair was perfectly parted on the side and, after looking closely, Dominick could see that the tops of his ears were definitely pointed. The man looked up from the tablet in his hands, smiling and waving in Dominick's direction.

"Mr. Bell. Welcome. I'm Harvey. Wonderful to have you."

"Hiya doing," Dominick nodded back as the other people looked his way, checking out the newest arrival.

"We're just waiting on one more person. It might be the afterlife, but we've found that even in death humans find it unnerving when stuff like this starts exactly on time. So, we'll get going in a little bit."

"As long as I'm not late."

"Never. Please enjoy the refreshments. We have some of the best discontinued snacks from the last fifty years. And bagels."

Dominick looked over at the buffet table. It had hot trays with bacon, eggs and warmed croissants. Trays of fresh fruit, and mountains and mountains of packaged snacks and drinks. He instantly spotted a Ninja Turtle Hostess pie. They were gone by the time he was after-school snacking age, but he'd heard rumors about them for years. He walked over and joined Coveralls, who was reading the side of a small box of Mr. T cereal. He set down the box and introduced himself.

"Talk about a strange turn of events. I'm Jeffery."

"Dominick, nice to meet you," he replied, shaking the man's hand before he nodded toward the crest on Jeffery's hat. "You work for the city?"

Jeffery nodded back, pointing his chin at the LAFD logo printed on the front pocket of Dominick's shirt. "Nothing quite as glamorous as the Los Angeles fire brigade. I'm in sanitation. Well, at least, I was. City of Pittsburgh."

"Trying to figure out where to start?" Dominick replied, reaching for the TMNT pie.

"I wouldn't do that just yet," Jeffery said as Dominick pulled open the wrapper.

"Is it all poisoned?" Dominick joked, as his fingers froze.

"It could be," the Asian guy said, appearing suddenly on his other side. "It's alternate universe travel rules 101. Don't drink anything and don't eat anything until you know it's safe."

Dominick looked down at the bright green frosting peeping out of the wrapper. "Fuck it. I'm already dead, right? If I double die, you'll know not to eat the food." He pushed the pie up a few inches and took a bite. He'd never had one when he was alive, so he didn't know if it was flavored with heaven dust or something, but that bite was good as a motherfucker.

"None of the food is poisoned, gentlemen," Harvey called out. "That's not how we roll around these parts. Also, it wouldn't make sense because you are, in fact, already dead."

Dominick shrugged and then turned back to the Asian dude and took another bite.

"Well, alternate universe rules 102. Someone should try the food."

Dominick patted him on the back as he took another bite. "We'll live to die again another day."

"I hope nothing is poisoned. I don't really want to go through that twice," a voice said from the door. Dominick looked over at a barrel-chested white dude with red hair and a red-blond beard, wearing a polo shirt and khakis that said he was a science teacher that also coaches football.

"Mr. Kiffen! Welcome. Please grab some refreshments and we'll get started. Everything is safe. I promise."

"Yeah, that's what she said," Kiffen grumbled as he walked over and grabbed a fistful of Kudos bars.

"Sweetie, did someone poison you?" the Asian guy asked.

"It's still pretty fresh so I'd rather not talk about it just yet."

"Guess I can't argue with that. I was relieved when I woke up here and not on a subway platform."

Dominick wanted to know if his new food-skeptical friend had been hit by a train, but Harvey cleared his throat to get their attention.

"Now that we're all here, let's get started."

Dominick grabbed a BoKu juice box, while the other guys made their own beverage selections, and then they all took their seats. He peeked into the mini Santa sack, which was actually empty. Next to it on the table there was a fancy gold pen and a leather-bound notebook with the letters D.B. embossed on the cover. He'd picked the seat at random, so maybe the initials were a coincidence? He looked over at Jeffery's notebook and sure enough it had "J.J." stamped on it.

"What's your last name?" he whispered, pointing to the leather cover.

"Jefferson."

"Hmmm."

"Just a bit of magic, Mr. Bell, and there's plenty more where that came from," Harvey said, making it clear he could hear everything they said from anywhere. "Gentlemen, I'm here to welcome you. My name is Harvey Gamarra. I am the local manager of personnel and you are indeed at the North Pole. While death is something that comes for everyone, we know the exiting can be a sometimes painful and confusing process. The door may have closed on your human life, but the five of you have been offered the opportunity of... this lifetime." Harvey paused and winked like he was waiting for applause.

"That was a good one, boss," Kiffen said.

"Thank you, Brendan. Now. The five of you are in the running for a very important position. We are in need of a new Santa Claus."

5

Tiffany went about her morning like usual. She sent the dogs out and, with Laurence gone, she refused to let any of the other animals in, at least for today. She needed to regroup. She knew some of the elves would be freaking out, even if they knew the vacancy would be filled soon. They were all smart capable adults, but they were also type A weirdos who liked their structure. They needed a Santa and she was going to find one, right after she took a nice hot shower and ate a quiet breakfast in her quarters.

When she was ready, dressed in her favorite off-day sweatsuit, she went to check on the children. Mrs. Fox and Mrs. Rabbit were waiting not-so patiently outside of her door, but as soon as they saw her, they seemed to relax.

"Ladies, I expected more from you," she teased before she headed on her way. They both followed and decided to stay with the children after Tiffany finished her rounds.

Tiffany knew Harvey had everything under control with the new recruits. He didn't need her at this stage of the process. They started with intake, a very long history lesson and then lunch. Still, this was her future partner they were talking about, so she wanted to check in on them anyway. She had the right to be nosy.

She made it halfway to her workshop, just past the crafting hall, when the unmistakable smell of sulfur filled her senses. She rolled her eyes and waited. A moment later, Krampus appeared just a few inches away from her in a cloud of dark smoke that would make a chimney sweep jealous. When the ash cleared, he was leaning against the wall, his obnoxiously spiked tail beating against the floor. Tiffany looked down at her nails, refusing to give him the attention he'd been trying to get from her for the last two centuries.

"What do you want, Karl?" She looked up at him as his serpentine tongue slid over his burnt lips.

"Same as always. Just a few moments to climb under that skin of yours and root around for a while."

"Ewww. My skin is gonna stay right where it is, thanks."

"Why won't you just give me a chance?"

"A chance for what? I don't like you, Karl. We just work together."

"Yeah and the last man you *worked* with just up and left you alone. A single mother needs someone."

Tiffany groaned, rolling her eyes. "Shut up. Laurence did not leave me. He was called for ascension by a loved one he'd been waiting for for a long time. I know you'll never experience that, but you know how it works. You try this every time. I'm not gonna let you set my hair on fire. I'm not gonna go on a weird date with you to a snuff brothel. You're into weird shit, Karl, and you'll never be my type, whether I'm in between husbands or not."

Karl's shoulders sagged and he had the nerve to look bashful. "Well, what are you looking for? I gotta talk to the new guys too. Maybe I can help you find the wrong man for you so you'll finally realize I'm what you need."

"Isn't there some corrupt businessman somewhere who wants you to chew on his toenails?" Tiffany asked.

Karl opened his mouth to answer. Thank god the voice of Tiffany's guardian angel, aka her assistant, came from over his shoulder.

"How long have you been here, Karl?" Shauna said, stepping between them, her tablet tucked against her chest. He was a frightening figure in theory, but Shauna shot him a mean stink eye, her nose ring gleaming.

"Ack! This is an important day. Big daddy Laurence flew the coop. I had to check on my lady."

"I'm sure. You have five two-minute appointments on the calendar and we shouldn't see you again until Veterans Day. Goodbye, Karl."

In a flash, he swelled in size and hissed in Shauna's face, baring his claws and fangs. She covered her nose until he disappeared in another thick cloud of smoke. Shauna threw a handful of glitter in the air and the smoke disappeared.

"I could smell him in my office," she said. "I figured he was bothering you."

"I thought about jabbing him in the eye with my fingernail, but he'd take that as foreplay," Tiffany laughed. "Thanks for rescuing me." Shauna had been with her for almost forty years. A former party promoter from Queens, she knew how to make lemonade out of absolute chaos.

"No problem. I thought maybe I'd see you sooner. It's a big day. A heavy day. An exciting day."

"I know and I know you love a debrief."

"And you. I wanted to make sure you were okay. What do you need? Is there anything extra I can help with?" Shauna asked. They continued walking toward the workshop. Tiffany noticed that, while music was playing and the general buzz of the Pole was still in the air, things were oddly quiet. No chirping birds, no squeaking mice, no scratching badger. They were all waiting.

"Right now, I need normalcy. But, I'm here if anyone on the crew wants to grieve formally. This is a first for some of them, including you," Tiffany said.

"Absolutely."

"Are *you* okay?" Shauna cringed and Tiffany couldn't help but laugh. "You do love a challenge."

"I'm sorry," Shauna replied. "Ruby gave me all her files on the last ascension before she left, but I thought it would be another three hundred years before I got to experience a new Santa selection process. I'll miss Laurence. He was amazing. I'm freaking pumped, though. We are going to find you a bitchin' replacement."

"I have no doubt you will."

"By the way, I'm loving the hair."

"Ugh, thanks," Tiffany said, stopping herself from fussing with it. "We're starting with it short this time. Laury was driving me nuts with the long shit."

"Why didn't you tell him?" Shauna laughed.

"He was the best Santa we've ever had. I wasn't going to argue with him over a bob. Which reminds me, I need to redo the bedroom and my office. I need to workshop ideas."

"Are we talking depressed and gentrified gray and beige or

over-the-top Black Friday in the world's tackiest Home Goods?"

"I'm thinking Nancy Meyers at Christmas doing an interview with the original Aunt Viv in a hidden gem Pottery Barn. Warm, but classy. I wanna pull back on all the red plaid."

"Perfect. I think this season is calling for blue, green and gold anyway. We'll transition to red ten days before drop to make sure everyone knows we mean business. I'll send over some bed frame ideas and it'll match your new desk."

"Love it."

"Well, we have all the candidates. Harvey's welcoming them now. Number five died just this morning."

"Oh geez. What happened?"

"Poisoned."

"By who?!"

"Who else? His wife. He didn't leave any kids behind, thankfully."

"Did he deserve it?" Tiffany asked.

"Come on. You know Oliver better than that. He wouldn't pick anyone who had it coming. She's cheating and didn't want to lose the house."

"Seriously, just get divorced. It comes with way less jail time."

"Funny you say that."

"Sweet cheeses. Tell me."

"Black widow in the making."

"Nooo!" Tiffany squealed.

"Our guy is husband number one. She takes out three more before her grown stepdaughters go full Cagney and Lacey on her and bring her down in about twenty-five years.

The cops don't believe them, but the girls get her confession on tape."

"Can Oliver do anything before she takes out three more husbands?" Tiffany knew a great deal about the universe and human existence, but a lot still made no sense. Miracles, divine intervention and all that, it happened from time to time. But, equally horrible and unfortunate, unfair things happened too. That's what made her job so important. She had to inject as much joy and kindness into the human world as possible, and depending on the social and political climate, her brand of magic was most effective a good three months out of the year.

She wasn't an angel, but she knew a few who did more than their share when the moment called for it.

"I mean, Oliver's on the stepdaughters, but Mom is already pure concentrated evil. No coming back from that."

"Damn. Well, at least he won't be counting down the clock to see her again," Tiffany said, letting an inside thought slip.

Shauna stopped in the middle of the corridor and turned to Tiffany. "Hey. Are you sure you're okay?"

"Yes, I'm fine. Laurence and I—it was the definition of 'you knew what this was'. I will miss him, but it wasn't *love*. It's fine. This time, I'll just pick the one who is clearly the best in bed and we'll make the most of it."

Shauna glanced down at her tablet. "I mean, we can make that a part of the interview process for those who are willing. Make things a little spicy. Consensual, but spicy."

Tiffany considered it for a moment. Sexual Olympic trials with five new people could be fun. But ultimately, she decided against it. As the thought left her mind, something else took hold. She didn't know what it was, but she felt a strange tug in her gut propelling her forward. She needed to meet these new men.

"Nah, it's fine. The suit, the bag, how he connects with the children and the elves. Heck, even Dasher and the girls. If we really connect, loins to loins, that's just a bonus."

"Sure, okay. You ready?"

"Yeah, tell me who we got."

Shauna swiped across her screen as they continued down to the southern portal. "Okay, first up we have Tyler Jameson Norwood. Twenty-eight. Child actor turned voice actor. Volunteers constantly at Children's Hospital. He passed four years ago. Accidental overdose."

"Hmm." Tiffany looked at his aging baby face and tousled black hair on the screen. The North Pole had plenty to keep the elves busy twenty-four seven, but they watched their share of human television too. She remembered him from a show the children liked, *Mikey Knows Best*. "Who's next?"

"Jeffery Jefferson—"

"Does he expect me not to call him Jeff Jeff?" Tiffany said. Shauna snorted in reply.

"He prefers Jeffery. Thirty-five. Garbage man from Pittsburgh. Never married, but he was in an entanglement with a woman he'd met in high school. Jeffery Jefferson died thirty-five years ago. Aneurysm. His lady friend has since moved on and married his best friend, who is her actual soulmate."

Tiffany looked at Jeffery's clean shaven, brown skin. He was handsome and he had a very serious look about him. That might be a good thing. For her sake, she at least hoped he had a sense of humor.

They rounded the corner, toward the southern portal's

opening. This time it was an elevator door. The two nutcrackers who guarded the exit stood there, sabers in hand. Tiffany stopped and urged Shauna to continue. She wanted to know about all of the candidates before she headed down. Shauna swiped her finger across the screen and a picture of a slim Asian man with a great head of hair popped up.

"Next, there's Christopher Ahn, aka MetroBang! A drag queen originally from Bartlesville, Oklahoma, but he moved to New York when he was sixteen. He spent most of his life as a social worker for the city, doing outreach with the homeless community. He was also one of the first drag queens to do drag story hour. The kids loved him. He died two years ago, saving an elderly woman from a flooding subway platform."

"So we're keeping him no matter what?" Tiffany said, not joking at all.

"God, I hope so. We need more queer New Yorkers around here," Shauna said before she moved on to the next profile. "Okay, next up, Dominick Bell."

Tiffany blinked when she saw the image of the brown-skinned Black man with a crisp fade and full mustache and beard. The broad shoulders were hard to ignore. "He's a looker."

"He is. Firefighter from Los Angeles. Thirty-six. Strong, silent type. A bit of a ladies' man, but respectful about it. He died last week. A reckless driver crashed into him on the way to a fire. Former foster kid. He was actually a safe surrender."

"Is that why he became a firefighter?" Tiffany asked. She could just picture all the firemen taking in young Dominick and raising him as their own, as a group. Like Twelve Men and a Baby.

"No. He likes driving trucks. He's been an engineer for Station 94 for the last five years."

"Oh, well we'll see how he does with the sleigh."

"Finally, we have our most recent addition, Brendan Kiffen. Who, as you know, was poisoned by his wife last night."

"Ugh, poor guy." Tiffany took in his thick, red hair and his bright blue eyes. If Dominick had broad shoulders, Brendan was *all* shoulders. He looked like a very big boy in his photo.

"Yeah. Thirty-four-year-old high school chemistry teacher and assistant football coach from Kennebunkport, Maine. He's been through it. His parents brought him up in the Light of God cult, which he escaped with his brother when he was fourteen. His brother went back and now runs the cult."

"Yeesh."

"Real stand-up guy though and, of course, great with kids."

"Okay. That's a good group. I think I can work with this."

"You wanna go meet them?" Shauna asked, just as Tiffany heard a familiar yipping down the hall. Mrs. Fox skipped toward them and hopped up on Tiffany's shoulder.

"Let's bring her," Tiffany said. "She sniffed out a real loser last time."

"Love it. Let's go." They turned back toward the elevators. The nutcrackers' swords parted and the doors opened. Shauna pressed the only button for the P Level and down they went.

6

Dominick quietly sipped his juice box as Harvey went on with his presentation. They'd gone around the room and done quick introductions. Harvey assured them they'd have plenty of time to get to know each other as the interview process went on. They all seemed like pretty chill, interesting guys, though the young dude, Tyler, seemed a little out of it. Not that anyone could blame him. They were all still processing their own deaths. Dominick was plenty confused, but he decided to just roll with it and see if he still had questions or lingering doubts when their boy Harvey was done. If this was all a dream, he'd have an interesting story to share with the internet.

"Now, I know you all have your idea of what Santa does. He's in the lab, making toys all year long and then he has twenty-four hours to hit millions of homes around the world. Talk about endurance, but there's so much more to the job than that. Before we finish here, I'm going to give you a rundown of the job and give a little history lesson about how the role of Santa came to be, how it's evolved to what it is now, and more information about the life we live here at the North Pole. After, I'll answer any questions before we move on to the next portion—oh my goodness!" Harvey let out a loud gasp and cupped his cheeks. "Isn't this a surprise."

Dominick turned toward the back of the room to see who or what Harvey was looking at. Two women were standing in the doorway, both Black and fine as hell, ears pointed too, but they each had a completely different vibe. One was tall and toned, with her thick natural hair shaved into a mohawk. She was wearing the same colors as Harvey, a glittery navy blue vest over a long-sleeved white shirt with holly and berries printed all over it, but she also had on black ripped jeans with safety pins and white marker graffiti all over them. Heavy black boots finished off the fit. She definitely knew how to pull focus, but Dominick almost let out a gasp of his own when he saw the other woman, the tug in his chest intensifying.

She had curves for days. He didn't like to be crass, but all his brain could process were thighs and tits and ass. She was thick as hell, wearing a red sweatsuit with pants that hugged her ass and bagged perfectly over a pair of white, fluffy snow boots. Her sweatshirt was cropped, hanging off her large breasts and showing off her soft belly. Her hair was cut in a cute-ass bob and her face? God, she was beautiful. Wide nose, full lips and deep brown eyes with long lashes that just felt like they were beckoning him to her.

That tug in Dominick's chest grew again, so much that he almost didn't notice the literal fox on her shoulder. Almost. The fucking fox was looking around the room like it was searching for something.

"I hope we're not interrupting," she asked in a husky

voice. "I thought we'd do things a little differently this time and I could introduce myself now." She bit the corner of her lip as she waited for Harvey's reply and Dominick had his answer as to whether or not he could get hard in the afterlife.

"You are interrupting and I love it! Gentlemen, this is a very special treat. I usually don't make this introduction until part two, but the lady gets what the lady wants. Please allow me to introduce Mrs. Claus."

Jeffery practically jumped out of his seat, taking off his hat. "Ma'am."

Dominick followed suit and stood as Mrs. Claus and the other woman started walking further into the room. The other guys followed, standing for the ladies.

"It's nice to see you all," she said, joining Harvey. "I know all your names, so no need to introduce yourselves again. I am Mrs. Claus, aka Tiffany Saint-Nicholas. This is my assistant, Shauna." She nodded toward the other woman who smiled and waved back.

"Hello."

"And this is Mrs. Fox." The very real fox jumped off her shoulder and took a long stretch and yawn break. "Please sit."

It was almost comical how all of them dropped their asses back in their chairs at her very command.

"I didn't get a chance to tell them about all the animals that live here at the North Pole," Harvey said.

"Oh yeah, we have a lot of animals here. It seems the kind of souls that are drawn to the work we do here are the same who commune well with nature.

"Like all your elves are Disney princesses?" Chris asked from across the room.

Tiffany laughed. "Exactly like that. You'll see."

"I was just going to dig deeper into Santa's role here, but please take the floor," Harvey said.

"I definitely don't want to derail your presentation, but there are a couple things I want to make clear since we're still on day one. I know a lot of you—if not all of you—are still feeling a little hazy or confused about your death, and the how and what the heck is going on here."

"You can say that again," Tyler grumbled.

Tiffany's nose twitched and her eyes narrowed the slightest bit, but not in annoyance or anything like that. Dominick could tell she was concerned. "There's rules to all this and I know the angels aren't allowed to share this part, so I'll tell you now. Everything is real."

"Can you elaborate a little?" Jeffery asked the question they were all thinking.

"Of course. Everything, and I mean everything, is real. This universe or this portion of it is connected to the human realm that you know. There are infinite realms, but here, our creator or God, whatever you want to call them, decided to let everything that humans could imagine become real. Heaven and Hell? Real. Martians? Real. Bigfoot? Definitely real."

Dominick listened, trying to wrap his mind around all of this. He had a bunch of questions, but he didn't know which one to ask first. He leaned forward a bit, intrigued, just as he felt something brush against his leg. He looked under the table and saw Mrs. Fox sniff up to his knee. When she seemed satisfied, she moved over to Jeffery and gave him the same sniff test.

"Tragically bisexual vampires?" Chris asked. "Are they real?"

"Very real and absolute trouble makers," Tiffany laughed again and Dominick suddenly felt a pang of jealousy. They got it. Chris could make her laugh. "Everything is real, including Santa Claus and his missus. Some entities exist on Earth and some, like myself and my amazing team of elves, exist in a space between planes and have the ability to go back and forth between them."

Brendan's hand shot up.

"Yes, Brendan."

"That Elf on the Shelf guy. Is he here?"

"Uh, no. That little narc works with Krampus, who is also real. You won't be meeting many other entities, but you will meet Krampus. He works adjacent to us."

"Does that mean Jesus is real?" Chris asks, hitting the real important question. "Ya know, since Christmas is your thing, but also his birthday."

"Jesus is real and he is hilarious and loves to cheat at cards. Actually, he cheats at everything, but it's funny when he does it and everyone is usually wine drunk. But even if you are selected to be Santa Claus, you might not meet him. He hasn't been to the North Pole in a long time."

Dominick raised his hand. He suddenly needed a very specific answer.

"Yes, Dominick," Tiffany said, and he knew that if they met in another lifetime, he'd instantly reconsider his low-commitment lifestyle just to hear her say his name over and over.

"I just want to clarify, uh, since you're calling yourself Mrs. Does whoever gets the job instantly marry you?"

"Basically. As Mrs. Claus, I am like the master of logistics. Santa Claus physically bonds with the entity known as the

Spirit of Christmas and is its keeper, so he's the master of vibes, if that makes sense. We need each other. The higher ups made a decision a long, long time ago that Mrs. Claus should be the permanent fixture. So yeah, I um—come with the job."

Dominick's eyes widened at the innuendo in her tone. Was she flirting with him? Might as well find out.

"And what happened to your last husband? What was wrong with him that he let you go?"

"It's kind of a long story, but our arrangement was not as trad wife as it sounds. We were both very busy, had a very healthy partnership and we parted on great terms. Someone was waiting for him in Heaven and when Gabriel sends a travel request, it's kind of hard to ignore him."

That only planted more questions in Dominick's head. He needed to figure out if he could get a few minutes alone with Tiffany so they could talk about this in detail. Landing the job of Santa was one thing, but the possibility of being with her for eternity? Gabriel really should have led with that.

"What happens if we don't want the job?" Tyler blurted out. "What happens? Where do we go?"

Tiffany jerked back like she'd been slapped. Jeffery made a grunting noise beside Dominick that said he was thinking about telling the kid to watch his mouth.

"Oh. Um—" Tiffany started.

"It's not you," Tyler replied. "I've just—I've been working since I was four years old and now I'm dead. I don't want another job. I wanna rest."

Tiffany's shoulders sagged, a deep look of understanding crossing her face. "I totally get it. Do you wanna go now or do you want to hang out for a while? We have tons of snacks."

Tyler didn't even look at the huge bowl of cheeseballs. "I wanna go now."

"No problem."

The other woman—or elf?—Shauna, pulled a golden phone out of her pocket and Dominick watched as she started texting fast as hell. A moment later, a golden door appeared in the corner of the room. It opened and smoke that looked more like clouds filled with rainbows billowed out. Jubilee poked her head out, a big smile on her face.

"Hi guys! Someone ask for a lift?"

"Yep," Tiffany said. "Tyler's had a change of heart. He's ready to go home."

"Great. Come on, your T.V. grandpa, thee Robert Craymore, has been asking about you."

Dominick wasn't shocked that tears filled Tyler's eyes. Someone important was waiting for him in a forever place where clouds came with prisms, the fresh scent of clean laundry and no stress from bills. It damn near brought a tear to Dominick's own eye. If he hadn't been determined to figure out more about this job and Tiffany, he'd hitch a ride too. Tyler thanked Tiffany and her two-man crew, took Julibee's hand and followed her through the door. In the next second, the door was gone.

Tiffany turned her attention back to them and Dominick couldn't ignore how hard she was working to smile. "And then there were four. And yes, it is that simple. Gabriel sent us his best candidates, but none of you are required to be here. If becoming Santa is not something you want, please let us know. A better place, a better fit is one call away."

"Anyone else want to bail?" Shauna said, clearly defensive on Tiffany's behalf.

"Nah. I gotta see this through," Brendan said. "I love Christmas. I was made for this."

"Yeah, I'm in," Dominick replied.

"Have to agree. I'm not going anywhere," Jeffery added.

"There's a fox in my lap, so I should probably stay." Dominick whipped his head around and, sure enough, Mrs. Fox was curled up, sleeping in Chris's lap.

"The hell?" he accidentally said out loud.

Chris shrugged. "What can I say? She senses the Disney Princess in me."

Tiffany laughed and Dominick had to remind himself that he'd never get the gig or get close to Tiffany if he choked Chris out.

7

"Well, Harvey. I think we've derailed your plan enough for one day. We'll get out of your hair," Tiffany said, trying to hide the wobble in her voice. "I'll see you all soon." She flashed the most convincing smile she could muster and very calmly headed for the door. Mrs. Fox had clearly abandoned her for Christopher, but she felt somewhat fortified knowing Shauna was just a few steps behind her. She kept her shoulders high until they were safe behind the closed elevator doors.

"Sweet Christmas morning. That was a disaster."

"It was not. You were great."

"Yeah, so great, one of our potential candidates was in a depressive stupor just begging to get out of here. Lost two men to ascension in one day. That's gotta be a new record."

"Tiffany," Shauna said, giving her a look.

"So what if I'm being dramatic. Leave me alone." The elevator doors opened again and the nutcrackers stepped to the side. Tiffany thanked them and started heading back to her office.

"Do you want me to yell at Gabriel? It's obvious Tyler wasn't a good choice. I'll give that angel a stern talking to."

"No. Tyler had a great spirit about him and I totally empathize. It's just—here." Tiffany liked to walk the corridors of the pole, be seen and available to everyone, but the nutcrackers didn't need to hear what she had to say. They'd tell the rest of their battalion that their fearless leader was doubting herself and the process. She snapped her fingers, and she and Shauna were back in her office. With a grunt, Tiffany dropped into her wingback chair. Of course, the first thing she spotted was the framed picture of her and Laurence sitting right next to her computer.

Shauna took her usual seat on the other side of her desk. "What's the problem? Talk to me."

"I think I just need a couple hours. End of day, even. I know we have to get on with the process. Winifred is already doing full prep and they launch Halloween in like a month. But seventy years was a long time."

"Tiff, he was your longest Santa."

"He was. You and Harvey have this under control. Take them through the rest of the training, introduce them around. We'll see how The Spirit and the children feel about them, and then we'll have our man." Tiffany knew that was a solid plan, but the look on Shauna's face said she didn't agree.

"You wanna know what I think?"

"Of course I do. That's why I pay you the big bucks."

"We don't have currency here, but okay. I think you are correct. You should give yourself your own adjustment period. You shared a life with Laurence, even if you knew he'd leave one day. You two were more than coworkers and we all saw it. Him just vanishing before you even get your morning bagel in is a lot to handle."

"Seriously. He could have let me get a latte first," Tiffany snorted.

"Rude as hell. But! I also just stood in a room with four *very* attractive men who made it very clear they are willing to give this a try. That means something. Also, I was going to wait to tell you, but two more creatures showed up today. I'm sure they'll be around to greet you soon, but they popped up at the same time, while we were in the elevator."

That grabbed Tiffany's attention. The animals came and went during spring and fall months. Two showing up at the same time in the middle of summer only told her one thing. There was a Santa among that final four.

"Well, that's good. I still need to catch my breath a little, though."

"Can you at least admit that you wouldn't be opposed to a D&B sandwich?"

"A what?!" she laughed.

"Dominick and Brendan."

"Shauna! You are nasty. Are those your top picks?"

"Honestly, I can't tell. So far, I like all of them, so I guess we'll see. Why don't you relax here? I'll catch up with Harvey and we'll make the necessary tweaks since Tyler bailed ahead of schedule. And then, I'll get started on the new designs for your quarters. While I'm doing that, I'll have one of the Sisters bring you up the sweet potato cake you like and some apple cider."

"Oh, that sounds good."

"Or maybe we can have Dominick deliver it with his shirt off?"

Tiffany winced. She'd had more than one inappropriate thought when she laid eyes on him and his very broad shoulders downstairs. "He is—that's a good looking man."

"So, make out with him. As part of the process, of course."

"No. This is serious. Get out of my office," Tiffany said playfully.

Shauna stuck out her tongue and started for the door.

"Hey. Before you go," Tiffany grabbed the framed picture and shoved it in Shauna's direction, "can you bring this down to the archive?"

"Sure."

"Thanks."

When Shauna left, Tiffany let out the most pathetic sigh. She looked at the empty space where the picture frame had just been. She needed to pull it together. No other entity had their partners hand selected for them. Finding a new Santa should not be treated as some sort of struggle. She was feeling sorry for herself. She knew it and she needed to knock it off. She'd end up with a great Santa, period. And she had plenty of work to do in the meantime. Tiffany woke up her computer and decided to look at what the elves had in mind for this year's craft fair, fully prepared to be dazzled to distraction.

8

Tyler's sudden departure, followed by Tiffany's, sucked the wind right out of Harvey's sails. To his credit, he didn't try to drum up the magic of Christmas to save the presentation.

"Why don't I show you gentlemen over to your cottage? You can get settled and then I'll swing by and pick you up in a couple of hours for lunch and a tour. I can do the rest of my presentation while we walk."

"Sounds good to me," Brendan said.

Dominick nodded and gave Harvey a thumbs up.

"Excellent. Gather up your things and follow me." Dominick grabbed his leather-bond notebook and his empty swag sack and fell in line behind Chris and his new animal friend, as Harvey led them to the hotel lobby. The front desk was still empty. When they stepped outside, a steam engine with two cars attached was just sitting there on tracks that were definitely not there before. Dominick didn't wanna say he felt a sudden wave of euphoria, but listening to the engine breathe and seeing the steam rise from the chimney had him a little choked up. He lived for heavy machinery and, while he'd seen plenty of trains and subways cars, he'd never seen a steam engine in person before. He really wanted a chance to operate this train.

The words *North Pole Express* were painted along the forest green car in white and trimmed with gold leaf. In that moment, he realized he'd never see Engine 294 again and it confused him even more that he was okay with that. It felt like this steam engine, and not the angels that had greeted him, really signified that he had moved on from the life he knew.

An older white man in a sharp navy suit and a conductor's cap stuck his head out of the cab window. "You gentlemen need a lift?"

"This is our conductor, Thomas. We don't always travel by train, but when we do, it's a good time."

"All aboard," Thomas replied with a bright smile. They headed toward the steps leading up to the passenger car. Dominick took a seat in one of the velvet upholstered booths. The whole space was warm and—dare he say—cozy, smelling faintly of sugar cookies that were still in the oven. Dominick had to stop himself from smiling, but he didn't know how long that would last. Chris dropped into the seat opposite him and Brendan and Jeffery sat on the other side of the car.

"What happened to the fox?" Dominick asked Chris, noticing his little forest friend was missing.

"She took off into the trees," he replied with a shrug. "Probably had an important meeting to get to."

"You'll see, the animals come and go, but they are all very friendly and welcoming," Harvey said as he took the seat next to Jeffery. A few seconds later, Thomas blew the whistle and they were off, chugging across the landscape. Dominick looked out the window, trying to nail down the scope of the place. When he looked back, the hotel they'd just walked out of was gone. It dashed Dominick's hopes of establishing a sense of direction in this place, leaving him wondering if there was any to be had in an intraterrestrial dimension between Heaven and Earth.

"Harvey?" he asked. "Are we on the same plane or whatever as the elves' compound? I'm not sure what you call it."

"We are." Harvey laughed. "When we get to the cottage, I'll make sure you have some maps, but if you look out the window, in a moment you'll see. We are right around the corner from Santa's village."

All four of them quickly turned toward the window as they entered a dark, short tunnel of evergreen trees. When they emerged on the other side, Dominick saw exactly what Harvey meant. An expansive, snow-covered village spread across the valley below. At first glance, the place had everything. Cabins and lodges. Storefronts with wooden sides and twinkling lights. A town square with a fir tree in the center that had to be as tall as a US Bank tower. Off in the far eastern corner, a row of large barns opened to an even larger pasture.

"Ha!" Chris shouted and pointed to the top of the other mountain rise. NORTH POLE was stamped into the side of the peaks in the exact style of the Hollywood sign. He looked at Harvey who winked at him.

Dominick focused back on the town square, making a mental note of where the skating pond was in relation to the bakery and the movie theater. As soon as he got a chance, he'd see how long it took to walk from end to end.

The train started to climb a steep incline and they went through another tunnel, this one seemingly made of gingerbread. It opened to reveal a two-story log cabin with a wraparound porch and an attached garage. Dominick hadn't spotted a regular road anywhere, but maybe there was some magical use for whatever was in there. The tracks curved right by the front steps and Thomas brought the steam engine to a smooth stop.

"Here we are, gentlemen. Your home for the next few days," Harvey said, bouncing out of his seat. He led them in a line off the train, waving goodbye to Thomas before the steam engine chugged into the snow. They continued up the stairs and Harvey opened the unlocked front door, which Dominick supposed made sense. The North Pole was probably more of a trust-your-neighbor type place.

The inside was nice, like the kind of place he imagined rich people stayed when they went skiing. It had a great room with an attached kitchen and a long dining table. Throughout, the walls were lined with all kinds of books, from thick encyclopedic volumes to paperback novels. Dominick was more of an audiobook guy, but maybe Brendan or Jeffery were big readers and that was for them. The fireplace was already lit without a screen in sight, which Dominick tried not to let bother him too much. Fire safety probably wasn't an issue here. And of course, there was a big flat screen T.V. on the wall, with several different gaming consoles neatly arranged on a wicker bench below.

"You each have your own room clearly marked," Harvey said, motioning around like a proud realtor. "You'll see that you don't need to sleep here, but we are connected enough to the human realm that the rhythms of day and night feel right. You'll take your meals down in the village, but the pantry is full of snacks and I know, Dominick, you and Chris are really good cooks, so feel free to whip up any snacks you want."

"Thanks," Dominick said, looking into the kitchen. He'd investigate the pantry later.

"Um, is there something we should know about this duck?" Chris asked. They all peered around him and, sure enough, a brown and gray duck with a flash of blue feathers along its flank came waddling around Chris's feet.

Harvey's eyes went wide and he dropped down into a squat. "Well, hello there." The duck let out a little quack and waddled right over to him. "You're new here, huh?"

The duck quacked two more times and it sounded strangely like he was saying yes.

"Welcome, my dear. Do you want to come back with me or stay with our new friends?"

Another quack and then the duck turned back toward Chris, stopping next to his foot before it started grooming itself with its beak.

"Like I said, animals appear from time to time."

"Should we all just give up now?" Brendan asked. "It seems like the animal whisperer here has the Santa nomination in the bag." Dominick couldn't argue with him there.

"No," Harvey laughed. "Chris is a wonderful candidate, but there is more to the selection process than the admiration of pond fowl. I'm going to pop back to my workshop for a bit, but before I go, I will ask all of you to investigate your swag sacks."

"Uh, mine's empty," Dominick said.

"Mine, too," Jeffery added as Brendan and Chris nodded.

"Have a little faith, gentlemen. Try again." Dominick headed over to the kitchen island as the rest of them set their red sacks on the dining table. He undid the golden drawstrings and peered inside. Something was in there, but he couldn't make out what. He put his hand in and felt something cool and leathery against his palm. He took hold of it and pulled out a vintage Dodgers letterman's jacket, blue with tan sleeves and the DODGERS logo stitched in white and tan across the back. He held it up by the shoulders, positive he was hallucinating.

He looked over at Harvey, who smiled back at him. "2014," Harvey said. Dominick knew the exact moment he was talking about. He'd been online and saw an old picture of Spike Lee in a director's chair, wearing this exact jacket. He'd looked around and found a replica on eBay for the low, low price of five thousand dollars.

"Thanks, man," he said to Harvey. He didn't mean to sound so choked up, but it was a dope jacket.

"Think of it as a welcome from all the elves."

Across the room, Chris started laughing as tears lined his eyes.

"What did you get?" Brendan asked him. Dominick didn't think any of them were expecting Chris to hold up a football. "Oh, I gotta hear this story."

The duck picked that moment to flap up on the table and give the football a close inspection of its own. Chris patted the duck on its head like they were old friends and let the duck sniff at the stitching a little more as he looked back at Brendan.

"What? You don't see how my move from wide receiver to

drag queen was a smooth and obvious transition? What you got there, big guy?"

Brendan reached into his sack and pulled out a huge box, too big to fit in a sack that size. "LEGO Millennium Falcon. Almost a grand after tax. I saved up for one and my wife used the money to go on a trip with her sister. Joke's on her, I guess. All she had to do was off me and I got it."

"Oh my god," Chris said, letting out a painful laugh. "Harvey, can we get this man an amnesia cocoa or something? Help the guy out."

"I'll be back soon," Harvey said, patting Brendan on the shoulder. "The cold won't affect you, but there are jackets and cozy sweaters in each of your rooms, along with a phone that will allow you to reach me. It also has a MAPS feature that will help you get around."

"Thank you for your help and hospitality," Jeffery said. The rest of them joined in showering Harvey with praise. Harvey just smiled and bowed with a flourish and then disappeared in a cloud of glittery smoke.

"Okay, so we agree? He's actually an elf?" Chris said as the glitter and smoke dissipated into nothing.

"Yeah. I think we can agree on that," Dominick replied.

"Hey, you wanna toss that pig skin around while we wait?" Brendan asked.

"Fuck yeah," Chris replied. "We can see if this duck can learn a zone defense." He tossed the ball to Brendan and they went stomping out the front door.

"You gonna join them?" Jeffery asked.

Dominick looked around, that tug suddenly pulling at his chest again. "Um, I'm gonna see what's up with the rooms first. You?"

"Gonna do a little research." Jeffery walked over to the bookshelf and Dominick crossed the room to see what he was reaching for. He pulled down a thick encyclopedia, *The History of Giving : VOL I.*

"If Tiffany was the deciding factor for this job, I'd say sign me up," Jeffery said.

"She is beautiful," Dominick said, trying to be cool.

"But I gotta know what I'm really getting into here, before I give up another few lifetimes or forever."

"No, that's smart. I'm gonna go find my room and the phone, and maybe I'll join you and see what I can figure out about the map."

"Good thinking."

Dominick grabbed his stuff and headed up the stairs. The top landing had a sitting area with a big window that overlooked the backyard. He could see Brendan and Chris passing the ball around and sure enough, that duck was gleefully running through the snow between the two of them. Dominick smiled, shook off the bizarre scene, and continued down the hall. Each door was labeled with a brass plaque engraved with their names. He found his, the second door on the left, and opened it. The room was nice, fancy b&b style with a large bed covered with a Christmas quilt and a bunch of pillows. The phone Harvey promised was on top of the covers.

Dominick set down his gifts and the sack, and snatched up the phone. He walked into the attached bathroom, weirdly happy to see the big shower and the claw-foot tub, but a little confused for a moment that there was no toilet. He remembered what Harvey said about being impervious to the cold and how they didn't need to sleep.

Clearly they didn't need to go to the bathroom either. Convenient.

He opened the double doors on the closet, found some very nice sweats and coats hanging up. Dominick grabbed a fancy, white high-necked cardigan and slipped it on for size. Of course, it fit perfectly. Looking in the mirror, he could see himself in an old R&B video, leaning against a window, singing about how he didn't mean to cheat, but he'd do it again. He walked back over to the bed and took a seat, checking out the phone. With a swipe of his thumb, it came to life with no lock feature, because who needs to lock their phone in the afterlife? He went to the contacts tab, suddenly disappointed that the only name in there was Harvey.

Dominick wasn't shocked by the thought that popped into his head, but he knew he couldn't do shit about it. He wanted to see Tiffany and he wanted to see her without the elf and his new band of brothers. He'd switched over to the map function, mentally sorting out what would be considered stalking, when he heard soft padding coming down the hall and the faint sound of a bell. A Dalmatian walked into the room and sat right in front of Dominick.

"Uh, hey. What's good?"

Obviously the dog didn't say anything.

"Did the duck send you?" Dominick joked and the dog barked. "Okay, then." He looked back at the map and its key, swiping over the candy cane icon for SANTA'S WORKSHOP. Maybe Tiffany was there, but the highlighted building was huge. No way he'd find it before Harvey was due back to meet them.

He glanced down at the dog and then back to the phone, another thing Harvey had told them popping back into his mind. "All the animals are friendly and welcoming," he said out loud. The dog clearly took that as a command, stepping a little closer and shoving its doggy head under Dominick's palm. He gave its soft fur a little scratch behind the ear and then took a gamble.

"Can you bring me to Tiffany?"

The dog jumped back toward the door, barking.

"I'll take that as a yes. Let's go." The dog turned and ran out of the room. Dominick followed, stopping quickly at Jeffery's room to grab his phone and rushed downstairs.

"Here." He set the phone on the table, next to the massive book Jeffery was engrossed in. "I'll be back."

"Where did that dog come from?" Jeffery asked.

"No clue, but it wants me to follow it." Dominick didn't stick around to wait for any follow-up questions. He yanked open the front door and followed the dog into the snow, the tug in his chest growing stronger with each step.

9

Tiffany was up to her eyeballs in quilt patterns and trim samples when she felt a strange sensation in her chest. She'd felt it earlier when she'd gone down to see Harvey and the new prospectives, but she'd chalked it up to nerves. Now that feeling was back, faint, but almost throbbing. She leaned back and stretched in her chair. She thought about taking a walk to the village center, just to get some fresh air, but decided against it. She'd have to stop every five feet and answer questions about the upcoming Santa selection. She was happy to answer questions in, like, twenty-four hours. For now, she still needed a break.

She turned back to her monitor just as she heard the doggy door in the wall pop up. She'd expected Shadow to come by at some point, but when she leaned back to look, a muzzle she wasn't familiar with peeked through.

"Hey. Who are you?"

The Dalmatian came over and sniffed her knee, letting Tiffany know in her telepathic way that she didn't have a name yet, but she was one of the new animals that Shauna had mentioned. Before Tiffany could do a proper introduction and line of questioning, she heard a knock on her door.

"Come in!"

Her door cracked open and Dominick Bell poked his head in. Tiffany hopped up from her chair like a nervous Jack in the Box, her cheeks warming all over.

"Mr. Bell. Hi."

"You can call me Dominick. Is this a bad time?" he replied, the bass in his voice making her knees tremble a little.

"No, no. Just surprised to see you. Come in."

"Thanks." He stepped inside, those broad shoulders of his taking up the perfect amount of space in her office. Gosh, he was handsome. Big and tall. Smooth, dark skin and a perfect beard and mustache combo. He was still in his fire station's t-shirt and the white sweater he had put on was really doing something for his biceps. She didn't let her gaze wander down to his tree trunk thighs, but she had a momentary thought of how nice it would be to drag her nails up the length of him. She was so hot and bothered, you'd think she hadn't been loved on in months. Laurence had taken care of her the night before, she just hadn't known it would be the last time. She'd never have guessed being across from one of the prospectives would ignite something in her so soon.

She swallowed and forced herself to remember who she was and who he was. What could he possibly be doing in her office right now? The new Dalmatian trotted over and pushed his hand with her nose, nudging him further inside. "I'm going, I'm going. Sorry. I followed her out of the house into the woods, through a portal, which brought us to an unlocked fire exit near your office."

"Yeah, no fires in a couple hundred years, but you can never be too safe. Have a seat. Tell me about your new friend," Tiffany said, motioning to the beautiful puppy. Later, she'd asked Harvey when they added that fire exit.

Dominick dropped into one of the chairs on the other side of her desk. "Yeah. Does she have a name or is this Mrs. Dog?" Dominick replied.

"Oh. Um..." Tiffany thought for a moment. She wasn't sure if she should explain exactly what was happening. She decided for a half truth, especially since she wasn't one hundred percent sure what the other half meant. "All the other dogs have actual names, but this cutie is new, so she doesn't have a name yet. Where did you find her?"

"She found me. I was checking out my digs at our visitors' cabin and she came strutting into my room. I asked her to bring me to you," Dominick said, letting that last word hang in the air between them. Tiffany swallowed, praying he couldn't tell that she was suddenly sweating. Magical immortal creatures such as herself did not sweat.

"Oh, well. You found me. Is everything going okay?"

"It's going pretty good. I think Harvey was a little shook up by the way Tyler dipped."

"Yeah," Tiffany said. "That was my fault. Kind of. Obviously it's very important to everyone that we find the right Santa, but I usually don't step into the process until day three. I jumped the gun today and someone dropped out. I should have just stuck with the plan."

"Day three is crazy," Dominick said.

"Why?"

"You're a very beautiful woman, Mrs. Claus, but you also seem like a pretty key piece to all of this. If I was on Earth applying to a job that came with loads of responsibility and a wife, I'd want to meet that woman first thing."

"Oh?"

"Yeah," he said. His tongue darted out to wet his bottom lip and Tiffany almost fell over in her chair. "I'd want to know if I was there to win the job or win you."

"Oh." Tiffany didn't mean to sound so breathy, but the word came out more like a sigh. A little part of her was begging her to tell him what she was really feeling. That she was still a little mixed up over losing Laurence, but she'd spent the last few hours coming to terms with the fact that she missed his companionship and she didn't know what she needed now. "On Earth that makes sense, but here, it really is about the job. We need a competent, capable Santa for the Spirit of Christmas to work. I'm not joking when I say humans need Santa, that's how much they believe in him."

"Hmmm," was Dominick's only reply.

"And here, the right Santa is like the molten core that keeps the North Pole alive. The elves, the children, the animals—"

"Children? You have kids?"

Clearly Harvey didn't get around to mentioning the children yet. If they were a dealbreaker for Dominick, she might as well know now. "Yes."

Dominick nodded. "I can support a single mother. What are they like?"

"Don't you want to know how many there are?" She almost laughed at the way he tilted his head. She wanted to remind him he wasn't required to pay child support in the North Pole. "Depending, there are between four and ten thousand children here."

"Come on, now!"

"I'm serious," she laughed.

"You do not have that many kids."

"I don't personally, but they are all under our care."

"Okay, you gotta explain."

"Well, you died, Gabriel gave you an opportunity to interview for this job. When children pass away, they get their own set of options, depending on their belief system. Some are reincarnated. Some are waiting for their Spirit to return. Some go straight to Paradise. We've found that most children develop lasting memories between ages three and five. So the kids here are between three and seventeen. But they came here for different reasons and are bonded to different people."

"So Santa has five thousand children. That's a lot of kids, Tiffany," he teased with this smirk that would be illegal back on Earth.

"No, actually. The reindeer and the elves are the leaders in guardianship. A lot of children love the idea of working at the North Pole, so they really look up to the elves. Santa has about a thousand kids. It's a breeze."

"Mhmm."

"You have to remember, Mr. Bell, it's all magic here and the magic makes it work. All you have to do is love them and show them you care."

"How many children are for you, Mrs. Claus?"

"You like calling me that," she said, flirting a little too boldly. She needed to pull it back, but she couldn't stop herself.

"Do you like it when I call you that?" he replied, nice and slow, and instantly she was wet. Tiffany looked down at her keyboard and tried not to squirm. It would just make the aching heat between her legs worse.

"We can't do this," she said.

"Why not? If I get the job, you'll be my wife. I want to know what my future wife likes. I want to know what she needs."

She looked back at his gorgeous face and failed at her attempt not to drown in those dark brown eyes. "That's not what this job is about. What we do matters. The holiday spirit is what keeps many people going some days, kids and adults alike. We need to deliver that. It's important, especially with so much evil in the world. It's not about me."

Dominick leaned forward and Tiffany hated how badly she wanted him to reach across her desk and touch her in any way he could. "And what if, to *me*, part of being Santa means really getting to know you? I'm not trying to be slick. Think about what you're asking us, Tiffany. Brendan got murked by his own wife. This job asks us to bypass an actual and real Heaven, and you think we're supposed to think you don't matter in that decision?"

"It didn't matter before. I shouldn't have said that. I'm sorry."

"What do you mean it didn't matter?" he said, jerking back. The sudden anger creasing his brow shouldn't have been a turn-on, but she could tell where it was coming from. He was worried about her.

"Nothing. I hear what you're saying. And yes, I do want to get to know all of you, but that doesn't mean you and I need to be here flirting our way into each other's pants. It's not a part of the process and, frankly, it's not fair to the others. They aren't getting one-on-one time in my office."

"Yeah, they are playing football and reading a book. I wanted to see *you*."

Tiffany let out a slow breath and swallowed. She could climb across her desk and straddle him. She could see how he would handle her large breasts pressed into his palms, pressed against his lips. She could test if he measured up to the very human hunger that still lived inside of her, no matter how deep it was buried. But, she stayed put.

"I appreciate that you came to see me, Dominick. Getting to know you is important."

"I'll back off. I just want you to know that I know that you know where my priorities are."

"I do," she laughed. "Thank you."

"So, there are two million children. How many dogs are there?" he asked, and thank god, because she'd completely forgotten they weren't alone. She peered around the desk and the lady Dalmatian was curled up in front of his feet, awake but definitely relaxed.

"Oof, I honestly don't know. Laur—the previous Santa and I had three dogs. Two of them went back to be with the children. My dog, Shadow, is around here somewhere. You'll meet her. But this little lady doesn't have a name yet. Since she came to you first, you wanna take a crack at a name?"

"Sure, I'll do the honors. Spot's too on the nose. How about Pepper? That's a nice pet name. I saved this old ass dog from a fire once whose name was Pepper."

"I like that. Pepper it is."

"Now that's that settled, I should probably get back before we give Harvey a stroke. Pepper and I went rogue."

"He lives for the stress and the excitement, but yeah."

"And I'm sorry I came on so strong," he said. "I just recently learned that life is, in fact, short."

"Gabriel told me that in death they allow for confusion, but not pain."

"Is there a difference?" he replied with a sarcastic smile.

"There's a big difference. One asks questions that should be asked."

"And what does the other one do?"

"The other one is why we have ghosts. And those exist whether humans believe in them or not. The pain makes it impossible for spirits to move on. I'm glad Tyler made it to this side. He's at peace now."

"Hmmm," was all Dominick said in return.

This time, Tiffany didn't stop herself. She stood and walked around her desk, careful not to disturb Pepper. Dominick picked up on what she was about to do and stood to meet her, opening his arms and letting her hug him tight. He was hugging her back, chest to chest, his chin resting on top of her head. She knew the flirting was dicey, but he deserved this. He needed it. She knew Gabriel and she knew death. Even if the role of Santa was an appealing offer, the transition was jarring in a way that was only experienced at birth. Dominick wouldn't hug most of his friends and family again, even if he did ascend. Hugging him to ease that shock was the least she could do.

She didn't expect the solid feel of him or his intoxicating, unique scent of wood smoke, currants, and pine. She didn't expect that tug in her chest to grow stronger too. It was human touch. She hadn't touched a human like this in years. They were still so close to the Earth, so vulnerable still that it pulled at something in her. That's what she told herself, at least, that the humanity in him made her want to hold on and never let go. She could at least admit that it was him that made her want to tilt her head up and find out if his lips felt as nice as they looked.

Tiffany took a step back and smoothed her hands over her hips. Big mistake. Dominick's gaze raked over her body.

"Anyway, no apologies needed," she said, clearing her throat. "Now I know more about you and you know more about me. If there's anything else you want to know, feel free to stop by again."

Just then, there was a knock on the door. Before it opened, she knew it was Shauna.

"Come in."

The look on Shauna's face was priceless. Pure shock and perverse self-righteousness.

"Hey, Shauna," Tiffany said.

"Hey, Boss. Dominick Bell. How are you?"

"I'm good. The new dog, Pepper, and I just took a little side quest. We're gonna head back to meet Harvey. I'll leave you to it."

"Okay. Thanks for stopping by," Tiffany said.

"Of course." Dominick moved out of the way so Shauna could come in and then held the door open for Pepper to scoot out. Tiffany waited for him to go, her nerves sparking, so Shauna could grill her, but he turned back, holding up his gold phone. "Hey, this thing only has Harvey's contact in it. Do you have a phone or a phone number, or should I just write a note and a bird will come bring it to you?"

Tiffany knew Shauna would never let her live this down, but she did what needed to be done. She snapped her fingers, then nodded at the phone. "Look again."

Dominick looked at his screen and the edge of his mustache lifted in a devastating smile. "Thanks." He closed the door and Tiffany could barely breathe. Shauna turned to her, her eyes practically bugging out of her head.

"Oh my god!" she mouthed.

"I know!" Tiffany whispered back.

10

Shauna rushed over and dropped down in her chair. "Tell me everything right now."

Tiffany stopped herself from patting her own blazing cheeks and sat back, trying to smooth out her breathing. She could still feel Dominick's arms around her.

"Nothing happened. The dog? That's one of the new additions. He asked her to bring him to me."

"Girl."

"Don't girl me. We had a very productive, professional talk. And I got to meet Miss Pepper. Dominick named her."

"Did she say anything else? Pepper?"

"Just that she's going to hang out with Dominick for a while."

"Girl."

"Stop," Tiffany laughed. "He seems... kind of intense, but thoughtful."

"And sexy. Don't forget sexy."

"Yes. He is very sexy." Tiffany cleared her throat and

nodded toward Shauna's tablet. "You were going to tell me something?"

"Nah. No way." Shauna's fingers started flying across her screen.

"What?"

"I'm telling Harvey on you."

"What? Nothing happened."

Of course, seconds later, Harvey's round cheeks appeared in her doorway. "Mr. Bell was here?"

"Frosty's beard. Come in and close the door." Tiffany held back a groan as her two best elves stared back at her, waiting for her to spill the beans. She gave them both a quick rundown of Pepper's sudden appearance and how Dominick had asked to see her. "I repeat. Nothing happened. He did allude to the fact that I—getting to know me—was a deciding factor in whether or not he pursued the position of Santa."

"And?" Shauna said, leaning closer. Tiffany hated that part of Shauna's job and her expertise as a friend was her ability to read Tiffany like a book.

"We may have flirted a bit. And hugged, but the hugging was only due to the fact that he is still struggling a bit with his sudden death, which is completely understandable. Maybe we should add hugs as part of our immediate intake. Tyler might have stayed."

"Tyler was not your Santa," Harvey said bluntly, in the tone he reserved for Christmas Eve, when he was not playing around.

"Clearly, but you sound so sure. You have some favorites? Holly Horny over here was already plotting erotic fantasies about Mr. Kiffen and Mr. Bell, at the same time."

"I do have favorites and I will be keeping those opinions to myself until the appropriate time. A very friendly mallard did appear and showed some interest in Mr. Ahn."

"Interesting," Tiffany said. "I can see Christopher getting along well with the children and the other elves."

"You should also see if he's good in bed," Shauna replied.

"I don't know how, but I'm gonna fire you."

"I have an idea," Harvey announced.

"Let's hear it."

"I think we need to change the process. I think Laurence was wonderful and it was clear to everyone in the Pole that he cared for you deeply. But, I think this time we need to find you a love match."

Tiffany looked over at Shauna, who leaned back in her chair, slowly crossing her arms as an extremely smug smile spread out over her face.

"We don't have that much time. How do you suppose we find me a love match?"

"I think that you should lead the process. I'll happily tag along—" Harvey started and Shauna promptly interrupted.

"I'm nosy. I want to come too. I have a vested interest as your assistant."

"Anyway! You were saying, *Harvey*."

"You lead the process and spend one-on-one time with each of them. Of course, we'll take all factors into consideration, but you give so much, if there is a chance to find someone special *for you*? I think we should take it."

Tiffany didn't know how to explain that that wasn't possible, on principle, but she was tired of giving her lecture about the job over and over. They just had to see for themselves. The requirements for Santa had nothing to do with her beyond the fact that they bond as friends and coworkers. All she needed was a kind companion, not a true love, end of story. But, she knew Harvey and especially Shauna were not hearing it.

"Fine. We'll do the process Bachelorette style. But if the Spirit doesn't approve of my love match, I don't want y'all to miss me if we both get catapulted into the sun."

"That's not gonna happen," Shauna said, grinning.

"What's first, Harv, sweetie?"

"I was going to take them to lunch and then start the tour. I'm happy to talk through all the history and things, but you should definitely lead the tour and the introductions, and then mingle with them as we go."

"Yeah, I'm definitely coming," Shauna muttered.

"Fine. I need some moments of silence to contemplate an outfit change."

Shauna sprung up from her seat and spun around. "Wear something trampy."

"I don't think trampy and Mrs. Claus go hand in hand," Harvey said.

"Thank you," Tiffany said. Of course, he wasn't fully on her side.

"How about something like this?" He waved his fingers over his tablet and handed it over. Tiffany looked at the cute, yet suggestive outfit. A tight red, long-sleeved hooded dress that fell about mid thigh, which on her really meant upper thigh when she walked. The hem on the bottom, the cuffs and the hood were lined with fluffy white fur. It was completed by matching fur-lined boots in white, similar to the ones she already had on.

"That's a date night situation and this is not a date. It's an interview. How about this?" Tiffany snapped her fingers then stood up.

"Perfect!" Shauna said. Harvey nodded in agreement. Tiffany knew she was going to regret this, but the faster it went horribly wrong, the quicker they could get back to the original plan.

11

Dominick had never gone on a clandestine mission through the woods or the snow before, but Pepper sure knew her way around for a fellow newbie. They came through the trees the same way they'd gone in. Dominick could still hear Chris and Brendan laughing in the backyard, so he was pretty sure they'd beat Harvey back. He followed Pepper up the stairs and shouldn't have been shocked that there was suddenly a doggy door cut in the log siding right beside the front door, but it was gonna take him more than a few hours to get used to the magic of this place.

He stepped inside and found Jeffery still at the table, more books stacked beside him. Jeffery glanced up before he reached down to greet Pepper, who was sniffing the cuff of his coveralls.

"Learn anything good?" Dominick asked. He pulled up a chair, pretending he couldn't still feel Tiffany in his arms. His chest swelled a little just thinking about her and the sweet wintry scent she carried.

"Yeah," Jeffery replied, as he flipped the cover of the current tome up so Dominick could see. "Apparently I—or we—can speed read here."

Dominick looked at the thick-ass books spread out in front of them. "You read all of these while I was gone?"

"Yes, sir. Covered about a thousand years of human history."

"And?" Dominick couldn't keep the shock off his face.

"It appears the Spirit of Giving is the main thing that stops civilization from crumbling. Yeah, the corporate machine wants us to celebrate the greeting card holidays, but gifts of harvest, livestock, all that, are as old as human existence. We've also been giving kids toys of some sorts since the dawn of time." Jeffery grabbed the first volume and flipped toward the front before he shoved the book in Dominick's direction. It had blocks of text and drawings, and museum-type photos of straw dolls and faded marbles. Jeffery tapped a specific picture of a wooden horse on wheels, then flipped to a short segment on the fable of the Trojan War in the middle of the book.

"We love gifts so much, they're one of the few things that consistently challenge our good sense of intuition. A giant horse or a poisonous apple. We love gifts."

"Hmmm, I never thought of it that way. We do or did the toy drives and all, but yeah. This is deep. Why do you look so stressed out about it, though?"

"You're not stressed out? This is a big job. And what did they give us this morning when we got here? Gifts. Now, I don't think it's nefarious or anything. I wanted that damn Slinky. It's just a lot to think about, the psychology and the necessity of giving."

"What were you doing driving a garbage truck, man?" Dominick joked. "I barely finished high school, so I know why I was a fire chaser, but you should have been a professor or something."

"Nah," Jeffery said, with a hint of a smile. "I don't care for people much."

"So what's the appeal of this job? Seems like we're gonna be dealing with thousands, if not millions, of people."

"I get the *purpose* of it all. You should understand that. It wasn't all fires, not even fifty percent of the time, was it? It was car wrecks, medical emergencies, cats up trees, teenagers stuck in toddler swings at the playground. Christmas parades. You were serving the people. You know how people learn to appreciate you after a garbage strike? I liked doing that service."

"Hmmm." Dominick almost felt bad for sneaking off to see Tiffany. Almost. But Jeffery did have a point. This Santa role had layers. He'd better learn those layers just as well as he wanted to learn his potential future wife.

"Where'd you and the dog run off to?" Jeffery asked. Dominick looked over at Pepper, who was snoozing in front of the fire.

"I just needed to get some air. I don't—I didn't have a sense of dying, so I'm just trying to wrap my mind around it." Which was mostly true. Talking to Tiffany, even if it was just for a few minutes—and that hug—helped.

"Yeah, apparently I've been dead for thirty-five years, but it feels like it just happened this morning. I feel like I should be pretty bent out of shape about it, but I'm not and that's confusing enough. A friend of mine once told me grief was for the living because there's peace in death. I think he was onto something because the last time I lost someone close to me, I definitely wasn't given a vacation and my favorite toy. A contemplative walk through snow sounds like a good idea. Come on, Dog." Jeffery closed the book and pushed in his chair, but Pepper didn't move.

"Oh, uh, her name is Pepper."

"Good name. Come on, Pepper." That seemed to do the trick. She trotted over and followed Jeffery to the door. After they headed out, Dominick figured he'd resist the urge to text Tiffany and do some reading of his own. Before he could start volume one, Harvey strolled in the front door.

"Mr. Bell. Just the man I was looking for."

"Here I am. Is it time for the luncheon tour?" He closed the book and started to stand, but Harvey pinned him with a hard look, which was interesting coming from an elf.

"Almost. I wanted to talk to you about the little detour you and your new canine friend just returned from."

"Oh. Was that not allowed? It was my idea, so don't kick Pepper out of this realm or whatever you guys do with animals that break the law."

"No," Harvey laughed."Pepper is here to stay. I just wanted to thank and commend you."

"Oh yeah?"

"Yes. You've changed our perspective on some things, so we'll be doing the process a little differently moving forward."

"And that's good?"

"I definitely think so. And no, I won't tell the others who you snuck off to see. They might see it as an unfair advantage in the selection process."

"Is it?" Dominick asked, jacking his own hopes right up.

"At present, possibly, but only time will tell. For now the secret is yours."

"I appreciate it." Jeffery seemed to be taking a practical approach to everything, so he probably wouldn't care, but the football coach and the drag queen, born competitors, might take that piece of information as a challenge.

"No problem at all. One moment, please." Harvey pulled out his phone and a few seconds later Dominick heard Chris yell, "Come on, Duck!" Chris, the duck, and Brendan came spilling in the front door, smiling and out of breath. Jeffery and Pepper weren't too far behind them. So much for his contemplative walk.

"Gentlemen, if you'll gather around, I have a little announcement to make," Harvey said. When the four of them, the duck and Pepper had his full attention, Harvey went on. "In the past, Mrs. Claus has left the selection process up to the angels, the elves and the Spirit of Christmas, along with the children who reside—"

"Wait, there are children here?" Jeffery asked.

"You elves using child labor?" Brendan added.

"No," Harvey chuckled. "There are children, much like us elves, who have chosen to spend their afterlives in the North Pole. Think of it as a forever Christmas break."

"How about we let our boy here finish his announcement and then we can ask follow-up questions," Dominick said. Harvey nodded his thanks and went on.

"Traditionally, we are given an order from above. We have to find a Santa, so we follow that selection process and it has always worked out. This time, however, we are going to do things differently. We have decided that it is important that Mrs. Claus finds a love match."

"Wait, she wasn't in love with the last guy?" Brendan blurted out. A question Dominick still wanted an answer to.

"There was much love between them, but Mrs. Claus's personal feelings were not taken into account during the selection process. Our previous Santas have excelled at the role and moved on when they were called to. This time, we are hoping the outcome will be different."

"Okay. So, what now? We all take turns speed running through a courtship ritual?" Brendan asked.

"I wouldn't put it exactly like that, but Mrs. Claus will be more involved in the selection process and we encourage you to get to know her. Truly consider if you can see a romantic future with her and she will do the same."

This was good news. Dominick could get closer to Tiffany without sneaking around, even if that meant the other men would get time with her too. Considering he was no punk, Dominick could handle a level playing field. Still, he had to know, was Tiffany the right woman for him and was he the right man for her?

"So, what do we do now?" Chris asked.

"Now, you will head to your rooms to get changed." Harvey gestured toward the shorts and muscle tee Chris was still wearing. "When you're ready, you will meet up with Mrs. Claus and go on what humans like to call a group date."

"You don't watch the Bachelorette up here, Harv?" Brendan said.

"I do not. But Shauna, who will be chaperoning the outing along with myself, gave me the rundown. Off you go. The ladies will be along shortly."

There was no arguing with that. Chris led the way as they all tromped up the stairs.

12

Dominick stepped into his room and found a blue Christmas sweater covered in small snowflakes and a pair of khaki pants folded neatly on the bed, a pair of winter boots on the floor at the edge of the rug. Pepper trotted in and hopped up on the bed. Dominick held up the sweater and looked at the red truck knitted right in the center with a chopped down tree resting in the flatbed.

"What do you think? Better than my uniform?" Pepper just huffed out a breath and rested her head on the covers. He figured that was all the input he would get. He changed quickly and tucked the Medal of Valor in his fresh pants pocket. He was sure Jeffery would have something philosophical to say about it being his talisman or something, but Dominick was fine with knowing he was keeping it on his person so he didn't lose it.

"Damn, I look good," Chris shouted from the hallway. Dominick grabbed his golden phone and headed out to find Chris in an almost identical outfit. His sweater was green with a snowman at the center.

"Very sharp," Dominick agreed as Brendan and Jeffery joined them, wearing the same khakis and a red sweater with a candy cane and a white sweater with a teddy bear respectively. They looked like a Ned Flanders holiday cover band.

"I guess this levels the playing field," Jeffery said, looking glad to be out of his coveralls, even though he still had his public works hat on.

"Well, fellas. This feels pretty official. May the best man win," Chris said.

"I'll make sure you're all invited to our wedding. Eat my dust!" Brendan turned and booked it down the stairs. Dominick took off after him, glad all his endurance training had carried over even in death. He caught Brendan at the front door as he yanked it open and pushed him out of the way, letting out a deep laugh as Brendan squealed. They both skidded to a halt, Chris and Jeffery bumping into them as they took in the ornately carved hay filled wagon, pulled by two powerful Clydesdales waiting at the bottom of the porch steps.

Harvey and Shauna were sitting up front with the driver. Tiffany was standing near the rear in an insanely tight, dark blue, velvet bodysuit trimmed with white fur. Dominick would be drooling if she wasn't standing there, clearly arguing with an eight-foot-tall, pitch black, hairy demon. It had horns, cloven feet, claws, fangs and a pointed tail. Its foot-long exposed dick was just hanging out there in between his legs. Nothing about him seemed like him belonged in the North Pole.

"No, Karl. Not now. Please leave," Tiffany seethed.

"Look," the demon said, pointing toward the porch, where Dominick and the rest of the guys were still standing, a little dumbfounded. "The gang's all here. I just wanted to introduce myself."

"And I said not now. Go home."

"Tiffany. Everything okay?" Dominick asked, starting down the stairs. He was pretty confident he couldn't take this Karl guy on his own, but maybe they'd get somewhere if the four of them jumped him together. Maybe.

"Yeah. Karl was just leaving."

"No, I wasn't. Hi, I'm Karl." The demon held out his claws for Dominick to shake. Dominick decided he liked all his fingers where they were and focused his attention back to Tiffany, taking a few not-so-subtle steps so he was standing in between them. Chris, Brendan and Jeffery weren't far behind, forming a tight circle around her.

"Aww, aren't they cute?Trying to protect you already. Boys, you don't have to worry. She's always safe against my capable tongue. I mean in my capable hands."

"Karl! You're gross! Go home!" Shauna yelled from the front of the wagon.

"You always this disrespectful to the missus?" Jeffery asked, putting some extra base in his voice.

"Yes!" Tiffany and Karl said at the same time. Karl seemed to be really proud of his sexual harassing ways.

"Just introduce me, Tiffy, and I'll be out of your bountiful cleavage."

"You are so annoying, Karl. And don't call me Tiffy," she spat.

"What's going on?" Dominick asked. The fire in her eyes seemed to extinguish the second she looked back at him, replaced by something equally as hot, but so much sweeter.

Dominick didn't stop himself from smoothing his fingers over her velvet-covered shoulder.

"It's fine," Tiffany replied, letting out a frustrated sigh. Her eyes narrowed as she glared back at the demon. "Guys, this is Karl, aka Krampus."

"At your service." Karl leaned into a deep bow, then snapped his tail against the ground. The sound split the air like a bullwhip.

"You were supposed to meet him tomorrow, for a whole thirty seconds. Unfortunately, we here at the North Pole work closely with Krampus."

"Doing what?" Brendan asked.

"A little of this. A little of that." A forked tongue lashed out of Karl's mouth. Dominick wanted to punch the shit out of him and throw up all at once.

"Karl taunts and torments a fraction of the small percentage of humans who actually believe in him. The children, he usually scares onto the straight and narrow. The adults—"

"The adults know what they like and usually come back for more." Dominick didn't have 'see a demon wink' on his bucket list, but there they were.

"And what does that have to do with the North Pole?" Jeffery asked.

"Most of the cultures that believe in him also believe in Santa Claus. We share our naughty list with him," Tiffany explained. "And even though we only need to meet maybe twice a year, Karl is taking advantage of the fact that there is no Santa right now to bug the crap out of me."

"I'm just trying to woo you while I have the chance. I

mean, you get me, fellas. You only get a chance at a creature this delicious once every hundred years or so."

"Goodbye, Karl!" Tiffany shouted. Dominick took a half step forward to give Karl some encouragement of his own, but the demon disappeared in a puff of dark smoke, leaving a deep echoing laugh and the smell of sulfur in his wake. Tiffany sighed again and leaned into Dominick's body. It felt so natural, Dominick wrapped his arm around her shoulder and pulled her closer.

"You okay?" he asked quietly.

"Yeah, I'm fine. He's just an ass. A persistent one, but he can't hurt me." She smiled and stepped out of his grasp, reminding Dominick that they definitely weren't alone. "You'll all get to talk to him one on one and you're welcome to try and fight him, but he might like it."

"Kinky," Chris joked. Tiffany chuckled and smiled a little wider.

"But enough about him," Tiffany said, flipping her fur-trimmed hood up over her curls. "You all look so nice. I feel overdressed."

Dominick shook his head. "You look great."

"Thank you."

"I was gonna give you a wolf whistle and a 'daaaamn', but it seems like Karl's skeeved you out enough for one day," Chris replied.

"Well, I appreciate being appreciated by pretty much anyone but Karl."

Suddenly Brendan was pushing his way between Dominick and Tiffany, taking her hand. "I'm gonna appreciate you then. Give us a spin." It was a bold move, but Tiffany seemed to be into it. She smiled up at Brendan and she slowly twirled around, letting him hold her hand above her. Dominick almost swallowed his tongue, looking at her curves covered in all that snug velvet. Chris let out a horned-up wolf whistle after all and Tiffany ate it up. Dominick had to figure out a way to get her alone again. This group shit wouldn't do.

"Karl should watch his mouth, but you look very beautiful," Jeffery added.

"Thanks, guys. You ready?"

"Where we off to?" Brendan said.

"We still need to give you a tour and Shauna suggested a hayride."

Shauna turned in her seat and flashed them all a big smile.

"Let's get this party started. After you, sweetheart," Brendan said. A wave of jealousy flooded over Dominick as he watched Brendan grab Tiffany by her waist and lift her up into the wagon. Brendan jumped behind her and followed her down to the end, so she was sitting right behind the driver, making it clear that Brendan was the only one getting close to her on this hayride. Dominick hopped up, trying to figure out the best place to sit.

"Here." Tiffany made Brendan scoot down a bit and patted the plaid blanket that had been laid over the hay bale beside her.

"Thanks." Dominick didn't waste the moment. He held out his hand, palm up, a little giddy when Tiffany took the invitation and laced her fingers with his. He just had to ignore the fact that Brendan took exact moment to swing his arm over Tiffany's shoulder.

Chris climbed up and sat right behind Shauna, across from Dominick. Jeffery slid up beside him. Pepper pulled up the rear, leaping in the flatbed and making herself comfortable between Dominick and Chris's feet. A second later, the duck flew over Chris's shoulder and took a seat right in Chris's lap.

"This is so cozy," Tiffany giggled. "I got four handsome fellas and two adorable creatures. We are about to have a time."

"Amen," Jeffery said.

Tiffany winked at him and turned back toward the driver's seat. "Guys, this is our friend, Franklin. He's been with us for about twenty years. Excellent driver and quite the equestrian."

Franklin turned and tipped his cap. "Are we ready?"

"I think we are."

"Away we go."

Dominick looked down as Tiffany squeezed his hand a little tighter. He looked over and realized her leg was shaking. He pulled her hand close and pressed a kiss to her knuckles. Chris noticed, but Dominick didn't care. Something was bothering Tiffany and he was going to find out what.

13

Tiffany was trying to breathe. She knew Shauna and Harvey would eat their words when this love match nonsense didn't work out, but she was fine with some harmless flirting while she led the tour. And that was all she planned to do until Karl showed up. She wanted to kill him, though it was physically and theoretically impossible. She could handle him normally, but that tug, the heat in her chest, seemed to have grown warmer when he appeared. It only grew hotter, almost pulsing, as they started to argue when her prospective Santas joined the scene.

She hadn't expected Brendan to be so forward, but she couldn't say she didn't like it, even if it wouldn't mean anything in the end. She also didn't expect to want to see Dominick again so badly, so soon. Focusing on the tour and their afternoon out seemed like the obvious move, but once they were all piled in the wagon bed, dog and duck included, she realized how little she was ready to pretend this was a good idea.

Tiffany liked to think she was hip and up with the times, but things had been so different when she and Laurence met. So old fashioned. She knew how the kids did things now, with the text messages and the situationships. She'd had confidence in her outfit before she left her office, but now she was actually nervous. The attention of four men at once was a little more than she'd anticipated. He'd surprised her, but she liked her short visit from Dominick. She should have insisted on seeing all the men one on one before they tackled this group outing, but what was done was done. Hopefully she'd relax by the time they got to the village.

Franklin smoothly guided the horses and wagon down the snow-dusted road. She could already hear the faint music coming from the village center in the distance, but Harvey had instructed the horses and driver to take their time. The ride was part of the date and he and Shauna wanted Tiffany to enjoy it. Joke was on them because she could barely breathe.

Her hand was warm in Dominick's, the feeling of his soft lips and the dark hairs of his mustache still lingering against her skin. She was a little flustered from the effortless way Brendan had hoisted her up into the wagon and she was happy to report that her sex drive was still alive and well, even if her nerves had kicked into overdrive. There were definitely worse places to be than between two bearded walls of muscle who were willing to get in Karl's face on her behalf.

"Are you okay?" Dominick asked quietly, as the wagon moved along. He pressed his leg up against hers, like he was trying to stop her fidgeting. When Brendan did the same on the other side, she knew he'd noticed her nervous tapping too. No way she was going to tell them the truth.

"Just excited. I've never been on a date with four people before."

Shauna turned around in the seat and Tiffany gave her a thumbs up with her free hand. Shauna snorted, probably thinking about how that D&B sandwich was closer to coming true, and then focused her attention on Chris.

"Does the duck have a name?" Shauna asked.

"I've been calling her Quackie O. She's been quacking at me, but I don't think we've sorted out the language barrier yet. I don't know if she likes it," Chris replied.

Quackie let out another loud squawk in the affirmative, giving all the magical members of their hayride a quick mental download of her thoughts on the name and the situation so far.

"She likes the name," Tiffany laughed. Even though they were all positive, she left Quackie O.'s initial thoughts on Christopher and Brendan out of the conversation.

"I'll take that as a good sign," Chris said and then he frowned, nodding toward Pepper's snoozing form. "Does the Dalmatian cuddled up in front of the firefighter mean anything significant?"

Tiffany felt everyone's eyes on her. Luckily, Dominick came to her rescue. "I don't think so. She ditched me for our boy Jeffery not too long ago. Probably just a coincidence she's a staple of the firehouse. Are ducks significant to drag in any way?" he said playfully.

"You'd be surprised! But no, I don't have any birds in my act. Just a lot of feathers."

"On that logic, this whole outing is catered to Dominick. Horse-drawn wagon," Jeffery spoke up, his tone a bit haunted and introspective. Tiffany looked over at him, unable to hide her shock. "Another nod to the fire brigade."

"Definitely just a coincidence," she said, quickly recovering with a smile. "We can teleport you guys around the Pole, but a hay ride seemed more fun."

"More romantic," Shauna said, jogging her eyebrows. That made Jeffery laugh and Tiffany finally exhaled.

"This is a great idea, Tiffany. Thank you," Jeffery said.

"You're very welcome. Next time, we'll bring the dog sleds," she said as Dominick gave her fingers another reassuring squeeze. She didn't look at him, but she returned the squeeze, trying to ground herself in the moment. As soon as she could, she wanted to speak to him alone, to thank him and maybe kiss him. "Chris, how'd you get started in drag?"

Brendan nudged her knee. "This is a good story."

Chris laughed and shifted Quackie in his lap. "Folks, let me tell you how badly things can go when you won't just let your son participate in musical theater." Chris went on to tell them how he'd been the youngest, with three sisters who constantly dressed him up and forced him to be their backup dancer when they were learning Christina Aguilera's choreography. He loved singing and dancing, and his parents were fine with him doing the occasional school play, though in rural Oklahoma he was usually put in the back somewhere.

"Things start to go really wrong in eighth grade. I get the role of Rooster in *Annie* and my mom tells me to watch the movie. And that, my friends, is when I figured out I was bi. Thank you, Tim Curry."

"God, he was so hot," Shauna added. Tiffany looked over at her and realized her assistant was enthralled by Chris's story.

"He was such a fantastic slut in that movie. Anyway, I leaned into that role a little too hard and then I started getting bullied for more than just being Korean. I'm walking into school one day and this kid, Mark Brevello, throws a football right at my head. I don't know if it was Gabriel's intervention or my Spidey senses kicked in—"

"He caught the ball," Brendan cut in, doubling down on his excitement about Chris's origin story.

"I caught the ball and threw it back. Our middle school and the high school were next door to each other at the time. The high school coach saw all this and bullied the middle school coach into bullying our drama teacher into bullying my parents into making me trying out for football."

"What happened?" Tiffany asked. They had Chris's basic bio on file, but it wasn't the same as hearing from the source. She was so fascinated by the way humans interacted with each other, especially children.

"I was on track to be one of the best receivers in the state, until I got caught with our quarterback, who was also our coach's son. Didn't go over well with the team, or my parents, or the drama club. They'd already cast the parts for the fall production, so naturally I had to run away from home."

"Naturally," Dominick said. Chris returned a smile to his teasing tone.

"My parents told my sisters to never speak to me again, but my oldest sister sent me some money and hooked me up with a brother of one of her college friends. He was equally disowned and doing drag in the Village. He taught me everything he knew and now I'm dead and riding in a wagon with you lovely people."

"I'm sorry about the premature ending, but we're happy

to have you," Tiffany said. "You know Shauna used to be a party promoter in the city?"

"Oh yeah?" Chris turned to Shauna with a big smile.

"Yeah, it was back in the eighties, though. A very different city. There are other Tri-State folks here, but not a lot of them were deep into the club scene."

"Nah, but that's cool. You gotta tell me about it sometime. Like, in the next twelve hours, just in case I get sucked into another dimension by an angel."

"I will, over lunch."

"We have to introduce him to Sister Peg," Tiffany said.

"Oh yeah! She's one of our bakery elves. She worked at Studio 54."

"Oh, I gotta meet Sister Peg."

Chris and Shauna continued talking about their adventures up and down the island of Manhattan, and Tiffany happily listened to them as the wagon crossed into the village. She was still a little nervous and she had no idea what and where they were talking about. Still, Christopher was very personable and animated. If he meshed well with the children, she could see him doing very well as Santa Claus.

"Where are you from?" Dominick asked quietly.

Tiffany almost jumped. It wasn't right for his voice to be so sexy. "Oh, um. I've lived in the North Pole so long, I guess I'm from here. What's the rule? Two hundred years or more and you can claim a place as your home town."

"I think at least one hundred and fifty years should do it." His warm smile melted her core again. She almost asked Jeffery if he'd played any sports as a child, but they'd reached the village.

Harvey had sent out a memo about this silly group date

and, at Tiffany's very firm demand, asked that the elves play it cool. It's one thing if your whole staff can't wait for you to find a new Santa, one who is competent and eager. It's a whole other thing if they're giddy for you to fall in love with him.

14

As they continued on, they passed Johnston, one of the wood cutters who was pulling a cart loaded down with fresh cedar. Mrs. Badger, Little Max and Little Cara in her mobility sled were tagging along with him. Tiffany wondered if she should stop the wagon and make formal introductions, but Johnston and the children just waved and kept on with their adventure.

"Firefighters have to learn how to chop wood?" Brendan leaned forward and asked Dominick. Tiffany looked between them as Dominick seemed to contemplate his answer.

"I know my way around an axe."

Tiffany was surprised she didn't combust right then and there.

Their first stop was at the stables. She tried not to think too much about how she missed Brendan's warmth or how she had to let go of Dominick's hand, so they could climb off the wagon. Jeffery helped her down with an efficient grip on her waist, but released her as soon as her boots touched the snow. She started to ask how he was doing when Brendan was beside her again, his heavy arm slung over her shoulder. She looked up at him, questioning, but he was looking at Harvey.

"Harv, I know you said you hadn't seen the show, but if we're doing this by Bachelorette rules, I'm taking my chance now." He looked down at her, his hand caressing her shoulder. "Can I steal you for a second?"

"Uh…" Tiffany looked at Shauna, unsure what to do. It didn't help that the other men, Pepper and even Quackie O. were looking at her, clearly waiting for her response. When Jax, one of the Clydesdales, looked back in her direction, she figured she should say something.

"Go," Shauna piped up, her tone light and not at all panicked. "We'll show these guys around and meet you by the reindeer paddock."

"Okay," she swallowed. "Let's go this way."

They turned and headed away from the barn. She didn't know what to make of the look she saw on Dominick's face as she went. Brendan didn't give her much time to think about it, taking her hand and leading her away, like he knew where he was going.

"Um, just up the left over here." They made it to the cove that separated the barns from the open pasture, which led up into the mountains. A redwood stump had been carved into an elegant bench, but Brendan took her over to the fence. A few of the black nose sheep were out enjoying the cold, but Dasher and the girls were still up on the hill. They'd wait until Tiffany called them down.

"It's a nice spread you guys have here."

"I like it. It helps that the animals take care of themselves. We have a few elves that work as their companions, but it's mostly because they were farmers when they were living and being down here reminds them of the best Christmases."

"Makes sense. Definitely wouldn't want to be up at dawn mucking stalls in the afterlife. We had horses, chickens, cows and goats. My father wanted us to have enough livestock for the apocalypse."

"Right," Tiffany said, her heart softening. "That must have been tough."

Brendan chuckled as if he was remembering something specific before he looked at her. "Are Dominick and Jefferson runaways too? Easier to deal with a Santa with no connections?"

"No," she smiled back. "I love that you are all trying to suss this situation out. The angels do the first round of picking. Maybe humans just have a lot in common."

"Well, I don't know anything about your last Santa, but I can make a case for myself. I'll be good to you. I'm hardworking and a fast learner. I'm good with kids. I raised my siblings, I was a teacher and a coach. And even though my wife killed me, I know how to treat a woman. She told me on our wedding day that I was so nice it was annoying."

Tiffany frowned, unsure if she should tell him the whole truth. There was no rule against it and he'd find out eventually. Still... "It wasn't about you, Brendan. What your wife did."

His expression dropped. "What do you mean?"

Tiffany told him what she knew, that his former wife would be brought to justice, but not until she'd taken more lives. "She's just getting started, I fear."

Brendan froze, a look of confusion and then relief passing over his face. "Oh. Well, that makes me feel better."

"It does?"

"Not for the other poor bastards, but now I know it wasn't personal. She's just got issues."

"Sounds like it. I am sorry, though." Tiffany eased her hand down his back in an attempt to comfort him. He turned to her and she thought he might go in for a hug, but he just looked at her.

"I meant what I said. I'd be good to you."

"I can see that."

"But there's three other guys."

"There are." And that's why the whole love match thing was a bad idea.

"Well, since we only have a few business hours to get to know you, you and I should probably kiss while we have some privacy," Brendan said.

Tiffany snorted. "Is that right?"

"Uh, yeah. How else are you going to decide? We're all smart. We're good looking. I know I don't compare to the firefighter with my shirt off and it might be inappropriate to tell you that I have an absolute hog between my legs. At least give me a chance to prove I'm a good kisser."

Feeling her cheeks heat, Tiffany looked around to make sure they were still out of sight of their little tour group. Brendan was forward, but it was surprisingly charming, and he did have a point. She'd had to teach Laurence how she liked to be kissed. It would be nice to know a little of what she was getting beforehand, even if it meant nothing.

"Okay, then. You can kiss me. Just don't get too handsy."

"I'll be on my best behavior."

Brendan closed the distance between them and cupped her cheeks in his large palms. He pressed his lips against hers, softly at first, then with more force and a probing push of his tongue. It was a good kiss. Good pressure, not too wet. When he pulled back, he kissed her quickly once more, like he wanted to be sure. Tiffany looked up at him. She felt a little warm and tingly all over, which was a good sign. She could work with that.

"Well?" Brendan said.

"Well, what?" She laughed.

"How was it?" he asked, his tone comically agitated.

"How was it for you?"

"Great. I was gonna really go for it and grab your ass, but you said to behave."

Tiffany considered him for a second, thinking about how little time they had. No one said she couldn't have a little fun with this.

"Hmmm. You can grab my ass if you can catch me." She started to back up as his brain tried to process what she was getting at. When the spark hit his eyes, she smirked at him and took off for the reindeer paddock. She decided to play fair. Brendan had no clue she could literally vanish between his fingers or that she could run as fast as light. She stayed just a few steps ahead of him, winding through the trees and slipping through his grasp the first few times he reached for her.

Soon, she doubled back between the fencing and a large cedar and let herself be caught. Brendan didn't grab her ass, though. He swooped her up like she weighed nothing. Her peal of laughter whipped through the wintry air as he kissed all over her face and neck, and then finally on her lips again.

Maybe she didn't need to pick a Santa. Maybe she could keep all four of them for different reasons. She could keep

Brendan for this kind of fun. He kissed her one more time before he set her down on her feet.

"You let me win, didn't you?" he asked, his cheeks as red as his hair.

"Maybe," she grinned, and then she shrieked as Brendan spun her around and slapped her on the ass. It was all in good fun and it would have stayed that way if she hadn't spotted the group coming toward them. She would have felt a lot better if her gaze hadn't been drawn straight to Dominick, walking her way and watching as Brendans stepped behind her and put his hands on her shoulders.

It should have meant nothing, felt like nothing. But, as soon as they locked eyes, that tug, that heat in her chest, was back. It didn't help that her dog Shadow had finally reappeared and she was walking right at Dominick's side.

15

Dominick had no justifiable reason to be jealous. Yeah, he clearly felt something illogical for Tiffany, considering they'd known each other for half a day. Still, seeing her up in Brendan's arms, giggling while he kissed her, had dropped a sour bomb in Dominick's stomach. He had enough sense not to crash out, but his eye might have twitched a bit.

Worst part was he only had himself to blame. If he hadn't snuck off to see Tiffany in the first place, the elves wouldn't have devised the love match group date plan. They were trying to create a level playing field because of a choice he had made. Now he had to suck it up and deal with the fact that Tiffany might actually be into Brendan.

Dominick kept it cool as he followed the group along the snowy fence line. He was happy to find out the black dog who had wandered up to him as Franklin introduced them to the horses was Tiffany's. Shadow and Pepper had circled and jumped around each other until Shadow barked and started backing toward the open doors, like she wanted them to follow. Dominick had to wonder if this was Shadow's way of cutting Tiffany and Brendan's one-on-one short. From the smug look on Brendan's face, it seemed like he got what he wanted.

Tiffany cleared her throat and plastered a smile on her face. "Look who you found," she said, squatting down. Dominick watched as Shadow ran into her arms. She wiggled around, letting Tiffany pet her before she dropped to her haunches and looked up at Tiffany with laser focus. Pepper trotted over and did the same thing. A second later, Quackie O. jumped out of Chris's arms and joined them. They were telling her something. It might have been a hilarious scene if Dominick had any idea what they were saying. And if Brendan hadn't inched closer to Tiffany and put a hand on her hip while she held her little sidebar.

"Didn't take long for him to get cozy," Jeffery muttered. Dominick couldn't tell if he was jealous too or just observing. He didn't think it was a good idea to ask.

"What do the ladies have to say?" Chris said, all loud.

"They're telling her we were right," Shauna chimed in. Tiffany glared at her, then turned her smile back to the animals.

"I hear you loud and clear. I'm on it," she said, before she looked up and waved the rest of the guys over. "I have a few special someones for you to meet. Come on." She turned and started walking into the open paddock, Pepper and Shadow falling into step beside her. Dominick followed, watching as Brendan tried to pull Tiffany close again. She slipped out of his grasp, then gave him a playful shove. He might have to say something to Harvey when they finally went for lunch. If each man had a chance to get to know her, that was fine, but this group date shit wasn't it.

Tiffany glanced back and caught his eye, her smile dropping. Dominick couldn't tell if she was suddenly embarrassed, remembering they weren't alone, or sorry that they had to witness her new connection with Brendan. He gave her a quick nod and a wink, letting her know they were still cool as they continued on. The trees started to thin and a wide swath of cleared land started its progression up into the foothills. It reminded Dominick of old abandoned runways in the desert. Tiffany cupped her hands around her mouth and let out a loud, high-pitched, melodic call. A handful of birds seemed to come alive throughout the forest and, a few seconds later, a long bellow came from the sky.

"Oh, that's chilling," Chris joked.

Shauna playfully swatted at his arm. "Just wait."

Suddenly the air started to stir. Something in Dominick's brain expected to hear the sound of helicopter propellers or the flapping of wings, but instead he heard hoof beats. He'd met with literal angels this morning. He'd met Krampus not less than an hour ago. Still, nothing had prepared him for the sight of reindeer flying in formation.

"Will you look at that," Jeffery gasped. Dominick glanced over at him, glad he wasn't the only one in awe. The dogs and the duck ran out to the middle of the clearing, like they were waiting to guide them onto the snowy landing strip.

Eight reindeer came to a gentle and easy stop, one after the other. They all gathered around the duck and Pepper, sniffing them from nozzle to webbed feet, including the reindeer with the bright red nose. The one that led the herd broke off and slowly made their way over to Tiffany, large antlered head bobbing.

"Hello, my darling. Thanks for coming back so quickly." She gently stroked down the reindeer's nose. "Gentlemen, I'd like to introduce you to Dasher." Dasher bobbed her head again and let out a deep, short mooing sound. Goosebumps broke out over the back of Dominick's neck just hearing it. "Jeffery?" Tiffany said.

"Yes, Ma'am," he replied, wonder still thick in his voice.

"Dasher would like to introduce you to her flock." Dominick watched as Jeffery swallowed and slowly made his way toward Dasher. She closed the distance and nudged him into the clearing with her antlers. Soon, all eight reindeer surrounded him, sniffing at him like they'd done to Pepper and the duck.

Dominick waited for some sort of jealousy to hit him, like it had when he'd seen Tiffany and Brendan together. A magical Dalmatian and a duck imprinting on you should have been a good indicator of your rankings in the Santa selection, but it was hard not to think that preferential reindeer treatment took the cake. Still, all Dominick felt was an intense sense of joy. That was the only way he could describe it. Flying reindeer were real. He couldn't put words to what that meant, but he felt something unlock in his memory just looking at them. Seeing them made him happy as hell.

One of the other reindeer looked away from Jeffery and made a similar mooing grunt.

"Okay," Tiffany said with a smile. "You guys can go join them."

Chris and Brendan rushed over, holding out their hands so Dasher and the bunch could pick up their scent, but

Dominick stood rooted in place. He felt like if he got any closer, he'd ruin the experience. Like if he reached out to touch their noses, all the reindeer would disappear. When Tiffany walked over to him, he quickly wiped away the tears suddenly lining his eyes.

"Are you okay?" she asked, giving his side an affectionate pat. Dominick wanted to tell her the truth, how rough his life in the foster system had been. How many years he'd spent shutting down different parts of himself, because no one was there to tell him what to do. How he'd shocked himself when he came out on the other side, able to care about people. Seeing Dasher and her crew confirmed that the soft parts of him that survived made sense. Somehow he still believed in magic.

He smiled at her and nodded. "I helped deliver a baby in the middle of the 405 once. This rivals that."

"They are pretty special. You should go over and say hello," Tiffany said.

"I will in a sec. I just want to take this in for a while."

He felt her relax, seemingly satisfied with his decision before she turned to him. "Hey, about before. With Brendan? I didn't want you to see that," she whispered.

Dominick waved her off. "It's okay. You have to make a choice. Why wouldn't you give him a chance? Plus, it looks like Dasher and the crew have already thrown their vote behind Jeffery. For all I know I'm in last place."

"I probably shouldn't say this, but no, you are not. I meant I didn't want *you* to see that."

Dominick glanced over at Brendan, who was asking Harvey about Rudolph's shorter antlers, before he looked back down at Tiffany. She had a pleading look in her eyes, like there was more she couldn't say. The pull he'd been feeling since he'd laid eyes on her seemed to pulse behind his ribs. He swallowed and lightly brushed her shoulder, like touching her would rein his emotions in.

"So you're telling me I still have a chance?"

"Definitely. Besides, for things to be fair, I have to kiss all of you, right?"

"Tiffany, please," he joked. "Not in front of the reindeer."

"Come on," she laughed, before she grabbed his hand and led him into the clearing.

16

Tiffany spent a little time with Dominick and Prancer before making her way around to see how Jeffery was doing. He was having a sweet, but intense conversation with Blitzen. Meanwhile, Brendan was loud talking with Rudolph, like he could understand a thing Rudolph was thinking. Rudolph liked Brendan, but he was only a few inches away, so he didn't have to yell. She made her way around to where Shauna and Chris were watching Quackie play a silly game with Cupid and Dancer. She knew Harvey and Shauna would want a full debrief at the end of the day, but this couldn't wait.

"Looks like all our furry and feathered friends are getting along," Tiffany said, giving Cupid an affectionate pat.

"Quackie is a duck for everybody," Chris replied. "Hey, you mentioned a former Studio 54 elf up in the place. Is there also a North Pole discotheque too?"

"We do have a great dance club in the village. Different theme every night and the occasional square dance. The elves love a square dance." Tiffany assured him. "I need to talk to

Shauna right quick and then we can head down to the village."

"I love a holiday queen with a plan," Chris said, offering her a high five. Tiffany laughed, slapping his palm in return before she gave Shauna the up nod to follow her. Even when they were out of earshot, she not-so-subtly stepped behind a tree and dropped her smile.

"This was a terrible idea," Tiffany hissed.

"What are you talking about? Things are going great!" Shauna replied.

"I let Brendan kiss me."

"I know. We saw." Shauna jogged her eyebrows like the little pervert she was.

"No, before that."

"So you kissed him twice. That's a good sign. Is he a good kisser?"

"What does that matter?" KISSING was probably item number nine thousand on her potential Santa's list of responsibilities.

"Um, if he's gonna be your husband, you should probably like kissing him."

Tiffany let out a grunt, realizing she had no ally in Shauna. "Look, I played along with your and Harvey's scheme—"

"Yeah, for a whole hour. You kissed Brendan and you had some quality time with Dominick. Just get some alone time with Jeffery and Chris, and then you can start weeding them out. Tiffany, you are thee Mrs. Claus. I need you to pull it together."

"I'll pull *you* together. I just don't like being the center of attention like this."

"Tough titties. You deserve love and we're gonna help you

find it. Plus, one of them will like this jittery side of you. That's your man."

"Mhmmm. What do you think of Chris?"

"Oh, I like him a lot. Good personality. Very funny. I definitely think he could bring the right amount of holiday cheer to this place. How are you feeling about Brendan?"

"Good? He's a little grabby, but it's kinda hot. And yes, he's a good kisser." Tiffany glanced around the tree. Brendan made her feel good, flirty, but she didn't feel like she was seeking him out. She looked around till her gaze landed on Dominick, who was standing with Comet and Donner, letting them sniff him. He looked up and caught her eye, his mustache lifting a bit in the corner as he smiled back at her. Instantly, Tiffany felt that deep tug in her chest again.

"But you keep thinking about Dominick?" Shauna said. Tiffany whipped her head back around.

"What? No! I was just thinking."

"Yeah, about how much you wanna let Dominick touch all over your body. It's okay if you pick him, you know. I heard what Shadow said. She went right to him in the barn."

"She did?" Tiffany gulped.

"Yep. She didn't even give the other guys a second glance." Shauna gave her a firm nod in reply. They couldn't tell the guys, but Shadow and Pepper were Team Dominick all the way. Quackie O. remained loyal to Chris, confident he had something special to offer to the North Pole.

"Yeah, but you heard what Dasher said. She's heavily leaning toward Jeffery. He's very serious, but he seems very thoughtful. We could use a thoughtful Santa."

"If he can drive a garbage truck, he can drive a sleigh,"

Shauna said with a shrug. "Well, you need to sleep with all of them, so we can clear up any confusion."

"Shauna!"

"What? You were thinking it too. Plus, I need to know if Chris is good in bed."

That gave Tiffany pause. Shauna and Chris had been orbiting each other this whole outing. She thought it was their New York connection, but maybe it was more. "Hey. Do you like him?"

"No," Shauna said, the surprise in her voice clear. "I mean, I like him as a person, but I'm trying to help you find a husband. Let's stop hiding behind this tree and take them down to the village and then we can arrange for you to get some alone time with each of them. Just to talk, not to fornicate. Let's see if you can get Jeffery to loosen up a bit."

Tiffany looked back toward the clearing. Shauna's plan made sense, but she still couldn't shake this nagging feeling. She couldn't admit that she most wanted more time with Dominick, either. If she told Shauna and Harvey, they would force them together. What if he wasn't the best choice for Santa, after all? She had the whole North Pole to think of, plus the millions of people who believed in him. They needed to make the right choice, which meant she had to put whatever was nudging her in Dominick's direction aside.

"Okay, let's go back. And no more talk of fornicating," Tiffany said.

"I am making no promises."

17

Tiffany was getting absolutely nothing out of Jeffery. When they got back to the wagon, she made a point to situate herself next to Jeffery on the hay bench. Shadow did her a solid and jumped up on the other side, to give her some space from Brendan's grabby attention. She liked that Brendan was making a sexy effort, but feeling her up was not Santa's main priority. She did not need to be horny right now.

Maybe it was silly to think that Jeffery would take this opportunity to do a little flirting himself, but all he cared about was logistics, which was probably for the best. His lack of interest in her was proving her point in real time. So far, it seemed like Jeffery would make a great Santa, whether he was interested in being her one true love or not. She might have to wait and see if he was okay with entering the kissing portion of the selection process.

"Harvey said almost all of the animals here are female?" he asked, scowling like his thought process was working overtime.

"About two-thirds. I'm actually not sure why. But, all of the reindeer with the exception of Rudolph are female. They used to be male, but humans realized that for reindeer to still have their antlers around Christmas time, they need to be female. The males shed their antlers sooner in the season."

"Interesting. And Rudolph?" he asked.

Tiffany shrugged. "The power of song. In the lyrics he's a he so he's a he here."

"Say that three times fast," Jeffery said, finally cracking a smile.

"He only guides the sleigh at night, but Dasher is their captain. Our Santa works closely with her on all of their flight routes." Tiffany explained.

"So the reindeer actually go out on flight missions?" Brendan asked.

"Absolutely. About five or six people across the world will see Santa and his reindeer streaking across the sky on Christmas night. The children will lock it away as a memory they could never get their parents to believe. The adults will believe and then convince themselves it's a hallucination. The hangar with the sleigh is on the other side of the village. We'll show you."

"Does the real Santa make any other public appearances?" Jeffery asked as they neared the village center. The lights on the evergreen hadn't been strung yet, but it still towered over the village skating rink, which was currently filled with children and workers on their break. Elves watched as they passed, offering warm smiles and waves of welcome, but everyone was self possessed enough not to rush the wagon. They'd get proper introductions soon enough.

"He does. He hits five different malls and takes pictures

for one shift each. Of course, he's just filling in for the guy who called in sick and he's the best Santa that mall has ever had, but they mysteriously never see him again." Tiffany almost told them about the time Laurence made a pit stop in Detroit and became a local legend for taking ridiculous photos with all the teens that jumped in line. "Even if the experience only sticks with a person for a few days or a few weeks, it can impact that whole year and it makes a huge difference."

"Hmmm," was all Jeffery said as the wagon rolled to a smooth stop.

Franklin turned around and addressed his passengers. "Ladies, gentlemen, dogs and duck. Welcome to Santa's village." They all thanked him and started spilling out of the wagon. Jeffery climbed down and offered Tiffany his hand, but as soon as she was clear of the backboard, he dropped her fingers and tucked his hands behind his back. He was definitely not as forward as Brendan, but that was okay. She could work with his interest in the details of the job, which the real reason he was here.

She led the group over to the village map in front of the General Store, before turning all of her Mrs. Claus charm up to an eleven. She couldn't help but laugh as Quackie and Pepper pushed their way to the front and sat at full attention.

"As Franklin said, welcome to Santa's village. Home to Mr. and Mrs. Claus, and all of the elves. Here, we are in the business of spreading love, peace, and a healthy dose of joy. The village center is where we meet up with our friends, dine, do a little shopping, a little dancing—" she held a dramatic pause, then winked at Chris, "and unwind, so we can do our amazing work, keeping the Christmas spirit alive. Some of our elves and kids have a wide range of disabilities, the North Pole accommodates all. If you look at the map, you'll see that the North Pole is laid out in a snowflake pattern along the valley and up into the foothills. Here we are," she said pointing to the map. "We are at the center. The workshops and our living quarters span out from here."

"Where are your living quarters?" Brendan asked with his eyebrow raised, bold as all get out.

"That is not on the map, Mr. Kiffen," Tiffany laughed. "But you'll see that my office and Santa's are at the top of the hill on the north end of the snowflake. We just came from the visitors' cottages here on the east end of the map and Santa's hangar is here on the west side. You have a full map of the Pole on your phone now and you are free to roam as you please. If you have any questions, the elves and the animals are happy to help."

Harvey stepped up beside her, clearly happy with her remarks. "Gentleman, we will give you a quick tour of the village center and then we've arranged for lunch at the best sandwich shop in the realm, followed by a taste-testing at the cookie lab."

"Now that's what I'm talking about," Dominick said quietly. Everybody laughed.

"You'll be very happy with the selection. Now, if you'll follow me." Their little tour group fell into step behind Harvey, but Tiffany had other plans in mind. She made her way over to Jeffery and gently touched his arm.

"We'll catch up," she told Harvey, who nodded in agreement before he told Shadow to take Quackie O. and Pepper down to the biscuit kiosk. She ignored the obnoxious smile from Shauna.

"Is everything alright?" Jeffery asked when they were alone. Or as alone as you can be smack in the middle of Santa's village.

"Everything is fine. I just wanted to thank you for your thoughtful questions during our ride over. I also wanted to ask how you are doing. A lot's happened."

"I appreciate that. I'm adjusting. Death, I can accept. I'm trying to wrap my mind around the vastness of the after. I started reading up on the history of giving before we left the cottage."

"So you understand why this is all so important?" Tiffany asked.

"I do. Dasher and I spoke, and she gave me more to think about."

"Wait. You and Dasher spoke?" Tiffany asked.

"Yes. She said I had the potential they'd been looking for. That's why they came back so quickly."

Suddenly Tiffany wished she'd spent less time freaking out behind a tree and more time paying attention to what was happening in the paddock.

"Can you understand the dogs? Quackie?"

"Yes, I can understand the duck. She's interesting."

"Huh."

"Is something wrong?" Jeffery asked, frowning.

"No. No! This is good news. We've never done the process this way before. Plus Laurence, the last Santa, met the reindeer on his own."

"Listen, I know I'm not as hot in the pants as Brendan, but it would be an absolute honor to be your husband. You are stunning and clearly very kind. I just need to consider the full breadth of the job."

Suddenly, Tiffany felt like her throat was going to close and her chest was going to collapse. Jeffery would make an excellent Santa, but it was a lot to hear Laurence's exact words echoed back to her some seventy years later. He'd taken the process so seriously and she had been an absolute afterthought. It had been fine and it had all worked out. If the children and the Spirit picked Jeffery, she knew it would work with Jeffery too. The fact that she could barely breathe right now wouldn't matter.

18

"Miss Tiffy!" Tiffany looked up at the sound of her name. The sight of Allie H. and Jessica P. running toward her wiped the nonsensical dread away.

"Hey girls!"

"While he was busy, absolutely hoarding the Spirit, Waltie said it was new Santa Day," Jessica said with an eye roll strong enough to power the sun.

"Is that true?" Allie asked, bouncing on the balls of her feet.

"Are the new Santas already here?" Jessica added.

"Girls, you're looking at one. Say hello to Mr. Jefferson. Mr. Jefferson, this is Allie and Jessica, two of our junior elves."

"Hi, Mr. Jefferson!" they said in unison.

"We're only sixteen, so they won't let us be full-time elves, but we're learning things," Jessica whined.

"Sorry if we don't want to give you full-time jobs," Tiffany laughed. "They are both learning from the pastry elves and they help out with the younger children. It's plenty of responsibility."

"It's nice to meet you both," Jeffery said, taking their high energy perfectly in stride.

"Why don't you show Mr. Jefferson down to the Ornament Emporium? You should catch up with the rest of the would-be Santas."

"Okay!"

"Come on, Mr. Jefferson."

Tiffany bit her lip to stop from laughing as the girls rushed him down the street, peppering him with questions. A few seconds later, though, the heft of this situation came rushing back. She was almost certain Jeffery would be Santa. That shouldn't have left her so shaken, but she wasn't ready for the selection process to be over yet. She didn't know why.

Tiffany made up her mind. She wasn't going through with this love match charade anymore. She'd excuse herself from the rest of the tour. Mrs. Claus had plenty to do all around the North Pole in the next few days, while she waited for the selection to be made. She'd accept whoever the new Santa was and they'd move on together.

A new sense of determination had her chin up and her shoulders back as she headed down the street. Shauna and Harvey would make a fuss, but she didn't care. As she got closer to the Ornament Emporium, she saw Dominick standing on the cobblestone street, looking at his gold phone, biceps bulging in his adorable Christmas sweater. Even though she wanted to go and see if she could get a little tag-backs on the hug she gave him earlier, she knew it was a bad idea.

She thought about using a bit of that Claus magic to poof

herself back to her quarters before he saw her, but the second the thought crossed her mind, Dominick looked up and gave her a sexy-ass nod before he smiled a little. She couldn't help but smile back as her traitorous feet carried her right to him.

"Mrs. Claus," he said, with that annoyingly perfect, deep voice.

"Mr. Bell. Not too into the ornament life?" Tiffany asked as he pulled her into a side hug. Not the bone-deep bear hug she needed, but just enough to feel the weight of him and not draw too much attention from the elves passing by.

"I was waiting to steal you from Jeffery, but he just went inside with the kids. Jessica and Allie? They said all the children were very excited that the Santa parade had started."

"Yeah. It's a big deal."

"I'm seeing that. So, what's up?" he asked. "I have nothing to go on, since I've known you for like five minutes, but you seem more than nervous."

Tiffany blew out a deep breath. Jeffery would probably be Santa in the next twenty-four hours and Dominick and the rest of the guys would be ascended. She'd never see them again. She might as well tell him.

"I think I like you," she confessed.

His eyebrows shot up. "Oh yeah?"

"You're calm and I feel like you're always keeping an eye on me."

"I am. Have you seen yourself in this outfit?" he teased. She nudged his hip.

"Stop it."

"I just feel—I feel this pull when it comes to you. I can't explain it. The magic of the North Pole maybe. I can be your man. Easily."

Another deep breath slipped out. Tiffany could see it too, but it didn't matter. "I know that Harvey and Shauna think they can change the rules and play matchmaker, but I've been at this a lot longer than they have. At the end of this, the North Pole decides. Not me."

"How about we just wait and see what happens. Maybe Brendan turns out to be an undercover demon and Chris discovers time travel and goes back. Also, I really want to kiss you right now, but—"Dominick looked around at the busy town square. "This probably isn't the right time or the right place."

Tiffany felt her cheeks warm at the thought of pressing her lips to his. "You can kiss me later. For now, I could go for a really good bear hug."

"Don't you mean a polar bear hug?" he said, wrapping both his strong arms around her.

"Oh no, he's corny," she giggled, as she buried her face against his chest. It should have been scary how easily she settled into him. It should have made her pause, this overwhelming feeling that Dominick Bell who barely knew her could give her the exact comfort she was looking for, that his touch was already something like home. She'd accept whatever decision she was handed, but it would be so hard to let him go when the time came.

"Hey!" Chris shouted, interrupting their perfect moment. Tiffany looked over her shoulder and saw him halfway out the door of the Emporium. "Dominick's gotta come see this."

"Come on." Tiffany took his hand, growing even warmer at the possessive way he intertwined his fingers with hers. Chris didn't seem to care. He was probably just excited to show Dominick the extensive ornament collection the Pole had crafted over the years. She followed Chris into the shop and darn near skidded to a stop when she laid her eyes on Brendan, crouched down in the middle of the shop on one knee, little Waltie standing beside him, talking his ear off.

All of that would have been fine and dandy because Waltie was one of Santa's kids. If any of them wanted the job, Waltie would get some say so, but it wasn't Waltie that almost had Tiffany slamming backward into Dominick. It was the fact that the Spirit of Christmas was glowing as bright as Christmas morning, perched right on Brendan's Kiffen's shoulder.

19

Dominick caught Tiffany as she backed into him. He held her close with an arm around her chest, as he tried to take in the scene and the strange levels of warmth and joy he was suddenly experiencing. Brendan knelt on the floor in the middle of the massive ornament display, talking to a small Black kid who couldn't have been more than six years old. He was cute as hell in a little winter coat and a knit cap, but the cuteness was overshadowed by what Dominick could only describe as a light phoenix. He wasn't deep into the lore, but a few of his buddies were into the *Lord of the Rings*. A creature that seemed like a fantasy from right out of that world, it was about the size of a bird and made of swirling light that seemed to emit emotion.

Dominick wasn't going to cry this time, but in some strange way, he suddenly felt like he could change the world for the better.

The little kid noticed Tiffany and ditched Brendan,

rushing over. Dominick gave them a little space just as Tiffany scooped him up and kissed both his cheeks.

"SC wanted to come down and visit," he said.

"Thank you for keeping her company today. That was kind of you. Did you introduce yourself to our new friends?"

"Yes. Mr. Harvey helped me."

"Good. This is Mr. Bell. Can you tell him your name?"

The kid didn't say anything at first. He just reached for Dominick, much to his shock. Dominick took the kid, who was definitely seventy-five percent down jacket.

"I'm Waltie. I'm five," he said, examining every inch of Dominick's face in that way curious kids do.

"Dominick. Nice to meet you."

"That's SC," Waltie said, pointing at the light show still swirling on Brendan's shoulder.

Tiffany looked up at Dominick, her eyes loaded with emotion that neither of them had time to process at this moment. "It's the Spirit of Christmas. That's a mouthful for some of the kids, so they call her Essee."

"I can dig a short form nickname. It's nice to meet you, Waltie. And Essee."

"You're welcome," he replied before he turned back to Tiffany. "Can I go play now? Essee wants to stay with you guys."

"Absolutely," Tiffany said.

"Thank you. Bye, Dominick."

"Bye, Waltie."

Dominick was about to set him back down, when Waltie leaned forward and whispered in his ear. "Essee went to Brendan first, but I'm one of Santa's kids and I think you should be Santa. We need a fireman." He leaned back and gave Dominick one of those *Can I trust you to keep this information to yourself?* looks. He couldn't let the kid's vote of confidence rattle him, but Dominick was definitely shook and more fully understood Tiffany's dilemma. It was any man's game and it didn't seem fair to make her put her heart on the line. Dominick gave Waltie a firm nod, which he returned before wiggling back down to the floor. Dominick tried not to laugh as Waltie stepped forward and addressed the whole store. "Goodbye, everybody."

The whole group and all the ornament-related elves returned his enthusiastic goodbye before he turned and ran out the door. One of the teenage girls, Jessica, playfully rolled her eyes and ran after him. Harvey had everyone's attention, explaining more about the way all of the stores in the village center worked. Brendan stood up and Essee followed, still perched on his shoulder. Dominick thought it was very interesting that they had an ornament archive going back nearly two hundred years, but he had more important things on his mind.

"Did you hear what Waltie said?" Dominick asked Tiffany, very quietly.

"Yeah, I did." She reached back and squeezed his hand. It wasn't a confident squeeze. It was a cry for help, searching for an anchor. Dominick squeezed her hand back and didn't let go. He could feel the anxiety coming off of her. He knew Harvey and Shauna wouldn't listen to him, and he wasn't entirely sure the Spirit of Christmas wouldn't melt his face off if he tried to get in the way, so the only thing he could do was stick by Tiffany's side. Literally.

"Just stay by me, okay?"

"'Kay," she whispered back. Dominick took a smooth step, so he was behind her again and wrapped his arm around Tiffany's shoulders, holding her tight. He knew that could have been seen as a blatant act of aggression by the rest of the fellas, and maybe Shauna, but he didn't care.

"Please explore the space and pick out an ornament that speaks to you. If you bring it to our lovely elves at the front of the store, it will be waiting for you back at the cottage. I can't wait to see what you find," Harvey said, dismissing them with a flap of his hands.

"You wanna come with me?" Dominick asked Tiffany.

"Yeah."

Chris and Shauna had already disappeared down one of the aisles and Jeffery, in his most grandpa-ass way, offered his arm to the teenage Allie, asking her to tell him more about her time since arriving at the North Pole. Dominick eased by Brendan, who was still vibing with Essee, leading Tiffany down the nearest section.

"Look, we'll check out some ornaments. We'll let Harvey lean into his true calling as a tour guide and get through the rest of the afternoon, and then you figure out what you want to do. I have no authority or power here, but I got you."

"I appreciate that, thanks. So what kind of ornament are we looking for?"

"I'll be real with you, I don't know." He stopped at some bright metallic bulbs covered with intricate, glittering designs. "Bouncing from house to house, you don't really settle into Christmas traditions. As a firefighter you get to do Christmas parades and stuff, but as a kid, I think I helped decorate one tree."

"I never decorated a tree either," Tiffany replied.

"Oh yeah? So, how did you get picked for the job?"

"Beat Krampus in hand-to-hand combat," she smiled. Dominick was glad this fucked up situation hadn't put a damper on her sense of humor. "No, I used to make toys. Dolls and rag bears. I was really good at it."

"Is there a toy archive here, too? I'd love to see your stuff."

A dark look passed over Tiffany's face before a smile that didn't reach her eyes snapped into place. "They only have one of my dolls, but I can show it to you."

"Can't you just magic your whole collection here? I mean, after meeting that duck, I feel like anything is possible for the folks here at the North Pole."

"Quackie is pretty special," she laughed, despite the darkness still hanging around her. "Uh, no. The elves offered to recover them all, but I told them there was no need. I made them for the Master's children and the children of other wealthy whites from Maryland to Virginia."

Tiffany almost sounded like she was bragging about the reach of her toy-making empire. Dominick had done the math earlier and assumed she'd been born before enslaved people had been freed, but he'd hoped she hadn't suffered that way. And now here she was, fighting her way through what would be her fourth magical marriage to a man she ultimately wouldn't pick.

"Tiffany, be real with me. Are you forced to be here?"

"No! No. At least once a decade, Gabriel asks me to come join his band of angels. It's a pretty sweet gig, but I love being Mrs. Claus. Heaven doesn't have stuff like this." She held up a glass slice of pizza with glitter pepperonis. "You think I'm giving up this kind of kitschy camp to deal with human problems? No, thank you. The doll they have in the archive is the only one I made for myself. She's the one I'm most proud of."

Dominick closed the distance between them and gave her a firm hug. "I'll be right back."

"Where are you going?" she shouted after him, but he just picked up the pace.

20

A few minutes later, Dominick had pulled Shauna away from Chris and wrangled Harvey outside of the Emporium. He turned on them, hands on his hips like he was addressing two reckless cadets.

"Pretty sure this is outside of my jurisdiction, but I don't give a fuck. Whatever you guys and the Christmas overlords are doing here, playing the *Dating Game* or whatever, it has to stop. Tiffany is miserable. And even if I am interested in being Santa Claus, I want no part of that."

"Mr. Bell, we know she's unhappy," Harvey replied.

"You do?" *The hell was wrong with them?*, Dominic wondered.

"Yes!" they said in unison.

"Just like the rest of you, Tiffany was once human and she came with her own very understandable trauma and baggage. She thinks she has no say in who Santa is, but that's not true," Shauna said.

"Explain some more," Dominick replied.

"When she became Mrs. Claus, things were very different

around here and so was she," Shauna continued. "She went with the flow, because why wouldn't she? She'd had very little choice in her human life. The first two Santas were kind and thoughtful. She got along with them and she was crushing it so hard with the elves and the children, those in charge decided to make her the anchor. When the Santas felt like moving on, they peaced out and she stayed behind to keep the North Pole running. Her last Santa, Laurence? She chose him, but for some reason, she thinks her opinion didn't matter because they weren't in love."

"Okay, I know it's none of my business, but what happened there?" Dominick asked. He didn't want to dig up Tiffany's pain, but she was keeping so much so close to the chest. He had to know what was going on.

"Laurence was great. The best Santa we've ever had. He was killed early on in the Civil Rights Movement, just a young kid trying to do the right thing. Three men were up for Santa that round and Laurence got it. Problem was, he left his high school sweetheart, Dottie, behind. Now, the universe can see backward and forward for a certain point in time, but free will is still a thing. When Dottie, this morning..." Shauna stared at him, giving Dominick a moment to remember how fresh this was for Tiffany too, not just him and the boys.

"I get ya. Go on."

"When she died, the only person she asked for was Laurence, so they could spend eternity together. And he went."

"Okay," Dominick sighed, trying to take it all in.

"Laurence had always been transparent about his human life, so Tiffany knew him leaving for Dottie one day was almost guaranteed, if he didn't just regular retire like the other Santas had. Problem was, Laurence was actually pretty great. She didn't fall in love *with* him, but she let it slip a couple times that she wished she was experiencing that kind of love with him or someone."

"In addition, Mr. Bell, the role of Mrs. Claus goes to someone who deeply appreciates that level of partnership. It is difficult for her not to have an assigned Santa right now. She feels like she is missing her other half," Harvey added.

"Right. Okay." This was becoming more complicated and Dominick wasn't sure how he should move next.

"We asked Gabriel specifically to find us candidates that had no romantic attachments on Earth. Jeffery and Tyler were so career focused, women weren't a priority. Brendan's wife unfortunately made her feelings known. She will be experiencing a different kind of afterlife and she was his only sweetheart. Christopher, in spite of his outgoing personality, has been guarding his heart very closely. He never found his special person."

"And you? I wouldn't say you're a ladies' man, but—" Shauna waggled her eyebrows at him. Dominick had had his fair share of sexual partners, but they were always on the same page.

"I have my own abandonment baggage. I can own that. But what do we do now, 'cause I don't like seeing her like this."

"Then get in there and woo her!"

"We can't pick favorites," Harvey said, "but we are encouraging the four of you to give her your best effort, if it's something you truly want."

"What do angels do, anyway?" Dominick asked, thinking of the parameters they'd given Gabriel and his crew.

"Ugh," Shauna said. "I mean, much respect, but I think it's a bummer of a job. You're answering prayers, performing miracles and dealing with the dead all day. I love humans, but they are awful to each other and it's hard to witness. I'd rather be an elf. Sorry."

Harvey nodded in agreement. "If you care about her, Mr. Bell, keep doing what you're doing. We're trying to show her that she can choose and she can be happy with someone who wants to give her forever. If this isn't for you, we understand and so will Mrs. Claus. Just like Tyler, we'll have Gabriel come scoop you up and take you right to Paradise."

It was a heavy sentiment, but Dominick could handle it. He was already dead. Taking a shot at an afterlife in this magical place with an even more magical, beautiful woman seemed like a pretty easy decision.

"We just want her to know that she can choose," Shauna said, "and the whole North Pole will back that choice. She's having a hard time believing it, considering Laurence left literally this morning. Time here is weird."

"Say that shit again." Dominick felt like he'd already aged fifty years, he'd learned and processed so much in just one day. He considered the elves in front of him for a long moment and thought about everything they'd said and what still needed to be done and decided. "I just have one request. After lunch, or after we finish the tour today, let's stop with the group date stuff. I think she's feeling a lot of pressure trying to split her attention between the four of us at once and it's not doing shit but making her feel guilty. She doesn't want to hurt our feelings."

They shared a look and after a second, Dominick realized they were using whatever telepathy they'd used to talk to the animals to confer with each other. Finally they seemed to come to a decision.

"We agree. Maybe if she spends more time with each of you one on one, she'll be a little more open to the idea of a love match," Harvey said.

"Great. And sorry for yelling," Dominick said, even though he'd never raised his voice. Having a six foot four Black guy tell you to get your shit together could be a lot for some people.

"Apology accepted. Now, get in there before Brendan starts another round of grab ass," Shauna said.

Dominick started back toward the Ornament Emporium, but he needed to know if he should punch Brendan in the mouth. "Did he grab her ass?"

Shauna just shrugged. Dominick rolled his eyes and jogged back inside. He found Tiffany alone, one aisle from where he'd left her. When she spotted him, she held up a shiny depiction of Santa in a fire helmet with a Dalmatian on one side and a fire hydrant on the other. It was cute, but he had more pressing matters to deal with.

"I don't know how much more time Harvey is gonna give us in here, so I'm going to say this right now."

"Okay," Tiffany said, sounding a little nervous. Dominick was determined to make it so she never felt that way with him again.

"I'm interested in the job. I want to know more about everything the elves have going on here. I want to hear more of Waltie's thoughts on pretty much everything. I definitely want to be able to talk to all of the animals. And I know when I get my hands on the sleigh? Oooh, girl." That made Tiffany laugh. "But, I need you to know, in no uncertain terms, that I want to do those things with you. I want to learn more about you. If I get the gig, I want to be by your side when I'm learning the ropes. Okay? If I'm going to be Santa, I want to be *your* Santa. That's the only way this works for me."

"Okay," she repeated, her already husky voice thick with emotion. Dominick stepped closer and cupped her cheek as tears started lining her eyes.

"If it's one of the other guys, I might cry a little on the way out, but I'll deal with it. But until then, I'm with you and that's all that matters to me."

"And the sleigh," she smiled as a few tears slid down her cheek. Dominick used his thumb to brush them away.

"I really want to see the sleigh and I want to drive that steam train too. And Franklin needs to show me how to work a team of horses. But after that, baby, I'm all yours."

"You really like driving, don't you?" she laughed.

Dominick closed his eyes and nodded. "Yes."

"Well, since you're so easy to please..."

Pretty confident he'd gotten his point across, Dominick pressed his lips against her perfectly soft mouth. She let out the sexiest gasp he'd ever heard and it took all his strength not to crush her to him. Her tongue slipped out and lightly brushed against his. His dick swelled and that lingering tug that had been in his chest felt like it had grown into a second heartbeat. A small voice in the back of his head made a big suggestion he couldn't ignore. What if his whole life wasn't about him joining Fire and Rescue? What if his life was bringing him right to the door of Tiffany Saint-Nicholas?

"Dominick, look," she whispered. Still holding her close, Dominick glanced over his shoulder. The Spirit of Christmas was slowly making her way toward them. Essee swirled over Dominick's shoulder and then around the crown of his head. Tiffany took a half a step back as the Spirit floated down in front of his face. A feeling of warmth and joy filled him from head to toe as he looked through the floating apparition. Tiffany's dreamy smile was visible through the other side.

Essee moved over to Tiffany and appeared to be whispering something in her ear, before she continued toward the back of the Emporium.

"Did she say anything?" Dominick asked.

"No, just that she's keeping a very close eye on things."

"Hmmm."

"Mrs. Claus! Tiffany!" Chris shouted from across the store.

"Yeah?" she called back, shaking her head.

"You gotta see this!"

"I should probably go see this," she shrugged, then slipped past Dominick.

"I'll be here, searching for the perfect representation of my life in a single item tied to a string."

"I believe in you," she laughed and then she shrieked as Dominick slapped her on the ass, encouraging her on her way. She shot him a shocked, but sexy smile. "Mr. Bell!"

"Look, I gotta keep Brendan on his toes."

Tiffany ran back and kissed him one more time. "Let me worry about Brendan. I'll be back." In a louder voice she said "On my way, Chris!"

She headed down the aisle. If Dominick hadn't been staring he would have missed the little extra sway she put into her hips.

21

Tiffany had to force herself to focus on what Chris was telling her. She could still feel Dominick's powerful palm on her behind. She could still taste him on her lips, smoky and sweet. She had no idea what had happened when he'd stepped outside, but Tiffany knew she would never forget the way Dominick had just spoken to her or the weight of his words. Laury had always spoken kindly to her. He'd always expressed his gratitude for their partnership, but he'd never made such a passionate declaration about anything, let alone her and her sense of peace.

The determination in Dominick's tone? He had no idea what it did to her heart. For the first time in a long time, she felt like someone really saw her. Tiffany. Not Mrs. Claus. Not Santa's wife. But her true self and how complicated her role was in all of this. Dominick Bell was special and, no matter what happened, she hoped she could keep him close. She and the North Pole needed people like him.

Blinking, she focused on the ornament just a few inches from her face. "Do you see that?" Chris said. Tiffany looked closer at the decoration, a simple snowflake made out of tongue depressors. It was covered in little holly leaves and berries drawn in magic marker. One of the stems had the name CHRISTOPHER clearly spelled out, but that wasn't what he was trying to show her. A little signature was on the back. Maya, with each A replaced with a heart.

"This is *mine*. My sister Maya made this for me when she was in third grade." His eyes shone as he spoke. Tiffany found herself choking up.

"Aww, Chris."

"Can I keep it? I was hoping to find something fresh and unique, but I don't think I can let this one go."

"Of course. You can pick out as many as you like. We never run out of ornaments."

Chris stepped forward and gave Tiffany a quick hug. "You know, Mrs. Claus—"

"You can call me Tiffany," she smiled back at him.

"Tiffany. I was gonna say, I really like it here."

"You do?" Tiffany felt her smile widen.

"Yeah," he said, leaning against the oak beam behind him. "I spent most of my life on edge and, at the same time, I was trying to make the best out of every situation. That's why drag worked for me. It was like a big distraction from the horrors of the world."

"I can definitely see that."

"But here, it's just—it's nice. I don't have to be the fun or the joy. It's already everywhere around me."

"See, that's basically the core of what we do here. Not to sound like I'm trying to lure you into a pyramid scheme, but it's true. We get Santa ready for Christmas night and we spend most of the rest of the year spreading joy in all kinds of ways. Tomorrow, someone will walk into a thrift store or go to a yard sale and they'll find a toy, a recipe book or an ornament that reminds them of one they had as a kid or something that used to sit on a shelf in their nana's house and it will light a little spark in them that has a ripple effect. Those things seem small, but they have such a big impact. Our elves make sure those little moments happen."

"That's actually pretty cool," Chris replied just as Brendan joined them.

"It is," Tiffany went on, rolling with it as Brendan moved past Chris and put his arm around her shoulder. "We've adapted with the times, and now we do things like test different cookie recipes, work on a new wreath arrangement or even revive an old one, and then one of our elves will find a human and whisper in their ear."

"So you're like the Christmas muses?" Chris said.

"Exactly. A few of the early elves *were* muses. They bounce around all of humanity. Things are a little dry for them right now. Turns out certain technologies and rabid hate make it hard for their inspiration to get through to humans, but I hear they're staging an epic comeback."

"Thank god!"

"Hey, is Cupid real?" Brendan asked. Just then, Jeffery and Dominick made their way over, ornaments in hand.

"Oh gosh, yes. Effective, but just as chaotic as the angsty bisexual vampires Chris mentioned," she laughed. "Cupid means well, but he's impulsive and sometimes misses his mark. But when he gets it right? Absolute fireworks."

"I gotta meet him," Chris laughed. "But tell me more about the inspiration sprinkles the elves fling to and fro.

"There's this influencer, ColorsThatPop, she's been

setting a lot of holiday design trends online the last few years. She has one of our best elves slipping her inspiration all the time. One of our senior elves helped with almost all of the successful Christmas ads from the nineteen fifties to the late eighties. So you see, it's a lot of work, but it goes a long way. So far that it can even loop right back to this shop." She pointed at the ornament Chris was still holding and winked.

"Well shit, I'm sold. If I don't get the Santa job, can I at least be an elf?" Chris asked. "I wanna whisper in some old lady's ear about holiday decor. I'll be like the elvish Martha Stewart."

"And you'd be amazing at it. I'll tell Harvey to put an asterisk right by your name. The rest of you find anything good?"

Brendan, with his arm still slung over her shoulder, held up a little Stormtrooper in a Santa hat, sitting inside a Christmas stocking. "I like Star Wars."

"Look, if you like it, I love it. What about you Jeffery?" It was freaking adorable the bashful way he held up his find. It was a four-pointed star with the Three Wise Men dangling below.

"I know you said Jesus doesn't visit very often, but I do love the Advent season," he said.

"It's a beautiful ornament and really, they were the OG gift givers. Everyone can learn a lot from them. Bring new mothers gold and smell goods. It's really that simple." Her heart melted a bit when Jeffery flashed what she was coming to realize was one of his rare smiles. She turned and looked at Dominick and the warm sensation moved to her belly and lower between her legs. He was sweet, thoughtful and too sexy for his own good.

"Mr. Bell, any luck?"

He pointedly looked at where Brendan's fingers were caressing her arm before he replied. He held up the ornament she'd picked out for him, Santa in the fire helmet next to the hydrant with his Dalmatian friend. "I decided to stick with this one and then I grabbed another one for the Missus." He passed her a hand-painted figurine of a brown-skinned Mr. and Mrs. Claus hanging from a gold ribbon. The Mrs. Claus was absolutely beaming as Santa pressed a sweet kiss to her cheek.

"Thank you, Dominick. I like this one a lot," Tiffany replied, underselling her true feelings on his thoughtful gift by miles and miles.

"Is there an official flirting contest we can enter, because I think Jeffery and I are behind?" Chris said.

"Hey. You snooze, you lose, big guy," Brendan replied.

"I don't flirt. I make my intentions clear and move forward accordingly," Jeffery added, in a rather gruff tone.

"I think what goes on between me and a lady is my business, even if you're there to witness it," Dominick added for good measure. Chris stumbled back in mock surprise, his hand pressed against his chest.

"Gasp. And I mean *gasp*. I enjoy a thorough read, but there I was, thinking I was amongst friends."

"He's right," Tiffany giggled. "You boys be nice."

"We are being nice. We're giving him a better understanding of the competition, so he can step his game up," Dominick said, giving Chris a playful nudge in the arm.

"Honestly, I'm surprised I found you two over here alone. This is the first time since we left the house that your head wasn't eight feet up Shauna's ass," Brendan said.

Things went still for a moment and Tiffany almost called Brendan out on his dig. There were jokes, but that comment felt like a low blow, especially when Chris had been nothing but an absolute sweetheart and Shauna was only there to help. She was still outside with Harvey right now, probably trying to work out the kinks for the rest of the day. When a sudden twinkle hit Chris's eye and a devilish smile spread over his face, she knew Chris had the situation well in hand.

"Well, if it's like that, Tiffany, Mrs. Claus, can I *steal* you for a moment?" he asked, staring Brendan down.

Tiffany snorted and used her own elf magic to poof out from under Brendan's arm. She reappeared beside Chris and slipped her arm through his before he even knew what was happening.

"Of course you can steal me," she said, pinning Brendan with a stern glare.

"Forgot she was made of magic and her own opinions, didn't ya, big boy? We'll see you fellas later." Chris turned and Tiffany let him lead her to the front of the Emporium. They left their ornaments with Sandy and Maxwell at the front and then ran laughing out the front door.

Shauna and Harvey were still talking across the plaza, with Shadow, Pepper and the duck milling around their feet.

"Hey, all done?" Shauna asked.

"You never saw us!" Chris yelled back.

"Come on," Tiffany laughed. Taking his hand, they hurried down the sidewalk.

22

Santa's village didn't have back alleys the same way a regular town did, so they made it around the corner and plopped down on a bench in front of Merry & Bright Coffee Co.

"That'll learn 'em," Chris said.

"Gosh, I needed that. Thank you."

"Look, it's been a day for all of us. Thank you for checking Brendan. Acting like he's the only dead guy around here."

"No problem. He might have a commanding presence, but he doesn't run things around here yet. I do."

"Yes, girl!" Chris cackled. They both sighed and fell into a companionable silence.

Tiffany eventually looked over at him and finally took the time to study him. Christopher Ahn was quite handsome. Everything about him was long and lean, the kind of physique that carried a surprising hidden strength. Eyes and hair, deep and warm dark brown. His smile was so infectious. He had a spattering of light freckles across his cheeks and the bridge of his nose. He was funny and very easy to talk to. Anyone would be lucky to have him, but she had to be honest. She felt nothing romantic for him. Still, she was very fond of him. Like Laurence, if he was chosen, she could see herself having a solid partnership with him, a good friendship that could grow to more over time. Worse things had happened. It was a perfectly acceptable conclusion and he was still a viable candidate for Santa Claus. And yet...

"Hey, I have a question for you," Chris said. He turned her way, draping his arm over the back of the bench.

"Sure, ask away."

"Do the elves have sex? Like, are people getting railed around here? Or is it all G-rated fun? I know Brendan decided to maul you right where the reindeer and my poor duck could see, but this is the North Pole."

"No one was mauled and yes, sex is allowed in the North Pole," Tiffany laughed. "All consenting adult parties are allowed to participate in consenting adult activities in the proper place, away from all little and reindeer eyes. You know the Church outlawed Yule celebrations at one point because there was so much debauchery?"

"Oh my god, that's sounds fucking amazing."

"My elves are doing it, trust me." *I'll be doing it again too, as soon as I'm Santa'd up again*, she almost said. Sex was very important to her.

"Glad to hear it. This place is too fun to be that dry," he said, before letting out a big sigh. Tiffany watched him as he leaned back against the bench and it felt like she was seeing a spent performer after their final curtain. She thought about what Tyler had said, before he'd headed upstairs with Jubilee, about how hard he'd worked and how tired he was. She thought about what Chris himself had said about how he'd had to move through his human life and how exhausting and isolating it sounded.

"Chris?"

"Should I give you a hickey to make Brendan jealous? Or should you give me one? He really did like throwing that football around with me. Who knows what would send him into a rage?"

"No," Tiffany laughed. " I don't think any hickeys will be necessary. I wanted to ask you a question. Do you—would you possibly want to be an elf? I think you'd be great at it. We'd still get to hang out and, while I don't think anything shady is happening with Shauna, I think you guys could be really good friends."

Chris winced, drawing air between his teeth.

"I don't mean that I don't want you as Santa," she rushed to clarify. "You'd be great at that, too. I just feel like the North Pole suits you in a larger sense. I think we both agree you'd be happy here no matter what."

"You're right about that, but Brendan might have been right about one other thing. I do have a little crush on Shauna."

Hearing it confirmed was a little odd at first, even if Tiffany didn't know why. She only had friendly feelings for Chris, but she felt that weird fleck of rejection, like he'd pulled himself out of the running hours ago. A voice in Tiffany's head jumped in quickly and reminded her that was a good thing. She and Chris were actually on the same page.

"I don't know how Shauna feels about this whole situation, but I'd be happy to be your wing woman."

"I'll talk to her. Maybe I should do like Dominick and handle my business like it's my business," he replied, doing a hilarious impression of Dominick's deep voice. "Do you really mean it? I can be an elf?"

"If that's what you want, yeah. We'd be lucky to have you."

"Then call me Buddy, 'cause I'm in. You have seen *Elf* haven't you?" he said, grabbing her hand.

"Yes. I've seen every holiday-related movie several times over." She pointed to the movie theater across the square. "So, it's settled then? You'll stay and be an elf?"

"Yes."

"Good." Tiffany leaned over and pulled him into a tight hug. She almost teared up at the way he hugged her back, like he could finally breathe, like he was finally home. She sat back and gave his knee a reassuring pat. "You can stay on the tour with the guys and then, in two days I'll send you off with Harvey and we'll figure out the right job for you. You can have your ears right away, though."

"Actually, can we hold off on the ears? I wanna mess with the guys a little. Make 'em sweat," Chris said. Tiffany sat back and listened to his plan. It was deceptive and a little mischievous. Tiffany loved it. After all, what was the point of being an elf, if you couldn't have a little fun?

"I love it," she said, once they'd hashed out the details. She pulled out her phone and sent Harvey and Shauna a quick text letting them know what was afoot, then she messaged Shauna separately, giving her a few extra details so she wouldn't get caught off guard by the first phase of their scheme. She messaged back right away.

!! !! !! I HAVE SO MANY QUESTIONS!

For later.

We're on our way with the boys.

"Okay, let's do this. They're coming." Tiffany slid across the bench, but Chris stopped her before she went in for the kill.

"Real quick. I know it's not my business anymore, but I just want to let you know that Dominick's your guy," he said with a whole lot of certainty.

"Oh yeah?" she couldn't hide her shock.

"I'll go into detail later. Now, kiss me like I'm leaving for war tomorrow."

Tiffany snorted and did just that. Chris was actually an excellent kisser. His lips were soft and the technique was solid. She took a few mental notes to pass on to Shauna before they were interrupted by a loud cough. Tiffany looked up and saw they were surrounded. It took everything in her not to laugh at the way Shauna and Harvey were holding in their own laughter. Brendan was fuming, Jeffery looked uncomfortable, like he wanted to be anywhere but near that bench, and Dominick squinted in their direction, like he didn't quite buy what they were selling.

"Oh, sorry," Tiffany said. "Are we ready to head to lunch?"

Chris stood and offered his arm to her. She stood and took it.

Harvey's lip twitched. Poor guy could barely hold it together. "Gentlemen, if you'll follow me. Sir McKellan is waiting for us with the best selection of gourmet sandwiches and sides the North Pole has to offer. This way."

As their merry party started off down the street, Tiffany reminded herself to properly thank Chris, her newest elf. She hadn't had this much fun in a while.

23

Chris and Tiffany were up to something. Dominick thought about getting to the bottom of it, but he had a feeling Tiffany would fill him in at some point. She strolled down to the sandwich shop, arm in arm with Chris, seemingly hanging on his every word as he told her more about his life. After they met the elves that ran the Holiday Food Emporium, they waited for their food in the cafeteria-style dining room. Dominick took a seat next to Tiffany, even though she was still chatting Chris up. He got the feeling they were both trying to get under Brendan's skin. Tiffany confirmed that fact when she slipped her hand over Dominick's thigh and gave him a reassuring squeeze as Chris chatted away.

He stopped his story about the time one of his more elaborate and expensive wigs caught on fire while he performed Phantom of the Opera at some rich lady's birthday party. Dominick's eye had twitched when Chris described how many lit candles had filled the cramped event space and he had to remind himself that his firefighting days were over.

They enjoyed their lunch of Thanksgiving sandwiches that Brendan insisted they all try and a warm apple butterscotch drink that was good as hell. As they ate, more elves and a few of the children came by to say hello. Tiffany assured Dominick and the guys that once the chosen Santa bonded with the Spirit of Christmas they would have the ability to speak any language, including sign language and the power to know everyone's name. So there was no need to panic if they met one hundred different elves in an hour.

When they were finished, they continued on to meet the elves who ran the cookie department, which was separate from the pastry department. Tiffany strode between Jeffery and Chris as their tour group crossed the village square, but Dominick's jealousy was in check. He knew what the deal was. Tiffany wasn't his girl yet, but he painfully wanted to be her man. It was hard to be near her and not touch her. He couldn't stop thinking about how soft her lips were or how good she tasted. How good she smelled. He wanted to be the one holding her hand. So yeah, okay, maybe there was a little jealousy and some possessiveness, but it was coming from a good place.

Dominick wanted to be the right Santa for her.

When they reached the Comfort & Joy Cookie Factory, she reached for Shauna's hand, then cleared her throat like she was about to make a big announcement.

"Alright, gentleman. We're going to leave you in Harvey's very capable hands. We just got news that a new elf will be joining us, so we have to get their start paperwork going."

"We have plenty to keep us busy, don't you worry," Harvey replied.

"Jeffery, if you're free, would you like to join me for dinner tonight?" Tiffany asked.

"It would be my pleasure," Jeffery said, offering her a little bow.

"Excellent. Christopher?"

"M'lady?"

The snort Tiffany let out confirmed things for Dominick. She and Chris were definitely up to something.

"Would you like to join me for brunch tomorrow?"

"You bet your boots I would."

"Wonderful. Brendan. Mr. Bell. I'll come find you sometime tomorrow evening. Until then."

"Bye!" Shauna said and the two of them vanished in a cloud of glitter smoke.

"Who's ready for cookies?" Harvey said all chipper, trying to salvage the situation. It was clear as Rudolph's nose that the reason most of them had been excited about this day out had just disappeared.

"I'm always ready for cookies. Come on, Harvey," Chris said, taking Harvey's hand. Brendan opened the door for them to skip inside as Jeffery followed close behind.

"She's really making us work for it," Brendan said as Dominick eased past him.

"It's not hard work for me, playboy," he replied, patting Brendan on the shoulder. Dominick decided it wouldn't be a good idea to laugh in Brendan's face as he let out an annoyed grumble, but he thought he'd made his point. Brendan was still in the running for the role of Santa Claus, but being kind of an asshole and a try-hard was no way to win an immortal goddess of the holiday season over. Flies with honey and all that, but Dominick was going to let him figure that out on his own.

They followed Harvey to the back of the enormous cookie shop, to an even bigger bakery. So far, every building seemed to have its own magical dimensions. Small and quaint on the outside, with the sprawling square footage of a warehouse on the inside. Like the cafeteria, the cookie factory had high ceilings with large skylights that were half covered with snow. Dominick missed Tiffany already, the smells of cinnamon, sugar and nutmeg enveloping him like a hug, even in the massive space. Maybe if he hung out with the cookie elves until she came back, he'd be okay.

They met with Sister Peg and an elf named Ernie, who were all ready to run the prospective Santas through a cookie tasting boot camp.

"We have a recipe archive of over ten thousand, dating back to the seventh century. And hopefully, by the end of your visit, we'll help you find your favorite," Ernie said, with a proud smile. "Follow me."

Dominick hung back and pulled out his golden phone. He sent Tiffany a quick text. He wasn't sure she'd answer, but it was worth a try.

I know you're busy with Human Resources,
but do you have a favorite cookie?

Tiffany responded before the screen could even dim.

Ask Sister Peg for cranberry oatmeal walnut.
It's heavenly.

Do you have a favorite cookie?

There was a joke on the tip of Dominick's fingers about sampling her cookie, but he suddenly remembered Miss Lara and her cookie shop down the street from the station. It stung a little that he would never see her again, but maybe he could pass on those good memories to Sister Peg and Ernie.

If your North Pole search engine has an earth directory check out Sugar and Salt in Los Angeles.

She has an espresso chocolate chip cookie that would get me through every tour at the station.

I'm on it.

"Dominick?" Harvey said. "Come on."

He looked up and their group was halfway across the bakery floor, gathered around a steel table piled with different cookies. Dominick jogged over and found a space between Ernie and Chris.

"Here are some of our favorites," Ernie went on, pointing to the left side of the table, before he gestured to the right. "And these are some of the humans' favorites from over the years. Cinnamon and chocolate are always fan favorites, but we find during the holidays, there's a boost in the popularity of almond and ginger flavors. Please dig in." Dominick looked across the dozens of platters. Gingerbread men and chocolate chip cookies. Sugar cookies with green and red M&Ms. Thumbprint cookies with a chocolate kiss in the middle.

Chris went right for some chocolate cookies that were covered in white frosting and sprinkles. Brendan went for spiral sugar cookies with almond slivers in them. Jeffery stuck with the classics and snatched up a perfectly decorated gingerbread man and bit one of the arms right off.

"Wow, that's good," he muttered to himself.

"Are there any cranberry oatmeal walnut?" Dominick asked.

"Of course," Ernie said. He reached for a small platter and held it up for Dominick to take his fill. "They're Mrs. Claus's favorite."

Dominick could see the appeal. He'd never been an oatmeal guy, but the cookies looked good as fuck. These elven chefs knew what they were doing. Before he could take one, Brendan's hand shot out and grabbed a cookie off the top of the pile. He was too busy eating to notice the way everyone, including the elves, marveled at his lack of home training.

"Damn. Tiffany's got taste," he said with a full mouth.

Dominick shook his head, then turned back to Ernie and thanked him before he grabbed a cookie of his own and took a bite. Tiffany was onto something. It was a good-ass cookie. Dominick made a mental note to find out her other favorite things.

"The holidays are the biggest cookie time of the year. The tradition of leaving cookies for Santa Claus started in the 1930s, so we've only been building up our cookie catalog over the last hundred years. Ah! And here comes one of our expert bakers now. Gentlemen, this is Lori-Ann."

Lori-Ann was a light-skinned Black woman with long micro braids. She was a smooth seven feet tall and it wouldn't have been hard to believe that she would have done pretty well in the WNBA.

"Hey guys! Miss Tiffany just sent down a new recipe.

Espresso chocolate chip. She said to make sure you get to try them."

"Thank you, my dear," Ernie said as she walked around with the platter. "An espresso cookie sounds perfect for a twenty-four hour sleigh ride around the world."

Dominick wasn't sure how she managed to pull this off, but when Lori-Ann reached him, it was impossible to deny Tiffany's big heart or the magic she held. The cookies weren't just made from Miss Lara's recipe, they were the same exact cookies. Dominick took a bite, soaking up the rich espresso flavor that burst on his tongue. He was definitely going to have to come up with a proper way to thank Tiffany.

"Oh, these are excellent," Harvey said.

"Yeah, these are good," Brendan added, his hands filled with other cookies.

Dominick watched as Lori-Ann produced a cream-colored note card with decorated edges from thin air. "The recipe is from Lara Adebayo, Sugar and Salt bakery, Los Angeles, California. Enjoy." She set the platter down and grabbed one for herself before she headed back toward the kitchens.

"Two great additions from Los Angeles in one day," Harvey said with a big smile and Sister Peg continued on with her history lesson. They sampled enough cookies to kill a man, but even after that big lunch, they never got full in any real way. They moved on to the research department where they gathered all their recipes and all the holiday memories that made those recipes special. When no one was looking, Dominick sent one more text.

How can I thank you for the cookies?

Another instant reply.

With your mouth. 😏

I mean! No thank you necessary.

And then, a moment later, while his brain and his dick were still trying to process that response.

Sorry. My extremely horny assistant was holding my phone.

I'm glad you enjoyed the cookies.

We can discuss thanks later.

In private!

Dominick hid his smile and slipped his phone away. He knew Harvey would keep them on schedule, but somehow he had to sneak away and see Tiffany. There had to be some magic somewhere in this place that would help him pull it off.

24

Even though Dominick was counting down the minutes till he could see Tiffany again, he had to admit the rest of the day had been pretty good. It was just *fun*. They ended phase one of their tour at the North Pole's post office, where they received millions of letters to Santa. Harvey really should have started there if he wanted to drive home just how important Santa and all the other residents of the North Pole were to the world. He was shocked by how many adults still wrote to Santa with manifestations, prayers or sharing their thoughts about the year that had just passed and the year to come.

It gave him a lot to think about over the next couple of days.

After Harvey sent Jeffery back—on a damn snowmobile—to get ready for his night with Tiffany, he released the rest of them to explore the North Pole. Pepper and Shadow were available to be their guides and, thanks to their secret mission that morning, Dominick knew Pepper could take them through the shortcut back to the cottage. They all decided to go see what was going on at the sporting lodge, when a group of kids showed up and asked them to come sledding. Dominick had never been sledding before, but Chris and Brendan assured him it was an experience he needed to try, especially since he was no longer at risk of any bodily injury or hypothermia.

Harvey poofed them into some retro snowsuits that had them looking like bullies from an 80's movie, but Dominick thought he pulled it off. They followed the kids out of the village center to their sledding hill, which looked more like it led up to the first base camp of Everest. Still, they easily hiked to the top, where they found a snack kiosk and a shed filled with sleds and inner tubes to ride back down.

At first, Dominick was mentally doing triage with every gravity defying maneuver. He had to remind himself that they were still in the North Pole and everyone was perfectly safe, even the smallest of kids who took reckless running starts and launched themselves off the hillside or the one kid he saw sliding down in his wheelchair. He finally relaxed when Waltie showed up and offered a bit of bravery.

"You've never sledded before?" Waltie asked, his voice filled with a bit of disbelief and disgust.

"Never. I'm from Southern California. It doesn't snow there."

"Okay. Well, hold my hand and go with me."

"Okay," Dominick laughed as the kid tugged him over to an available sled. Waltie took the driver's seat and off they went, flying down the hill. Dominick knew that a rush of adrenaline could come in all kinds of different flavors, but the cool air on his face, the wind rushing by his ears and Waltie's peal of laughter? This was the best, hands down, and they hadn't even reached the bottom. Chris was right behind them on an inner tube, a little girl named Olivia and that duck in his lap, laughing and screaming and quacking all the way. As they helped the kids trudge back up the hill, Brendan came flying down on a damn toboggan, three big kids and two little ones stacked up behind him, screaming their heads off. Maybe the funniest thing Dominick had ever seen.

They spent all afternoon up there, more kids, elves and woodland creatures showing up to join in as the day wore on. Rudolph and three other reindeer landed at the bottom of the hill and gave the smaller kids rides back up over and over.

At one point, Dominick stopped at the top and talked a little with one of the carpenter elves, Raymond. He was telling him how many kids arrived or ascended per year. "They decide to move on, or the parents or sibling they've been waiting for finally passes and they go to be with them. So, we build fresh sleds and fresh toys for the new kids who take their place."

Dominick looked down the hill, where Chris was in the middle of a pretty intense snowball war with some of the teenagers.

"It's a part of life. As you know," Raymond went on, like he was reading Dominick's mind, "some of us grow old and some die way too young. But we're here and, as you can see, the kids are happy."

"Yeah, there's no denying that." He spotted Pepper and Shadow using their doggy strength to tug a sled full of laughing and screaming little ones back uphill. He was about to ask Raymond how long he'd been in the North Pole when little fingers latched onto his gloved hand. He looked down at a six or seven year old Black girl who was surveying the chaos going on up and down the mountain. She was in a pink and red snowsuit of her own and her hair was braided up into two puffs.

Dominick glanced around, looking for a free sled. "You want me to ride down with you?" he asked her.

"That's Farrah the fifth," Raymond whispered. "We have a bunch of Farrahs. She'd be one of yours."

"Thanks. You want to do some sledding, Farrah Part Five?"

The little girl looked up at him and shook her head, before she went back to scoping out the scene.

"You wanna hang out with me?"

Farrah Five looked up at him one more time, nodding.

"Alright." He resumed his conversation with Raymond, talking more about humans and their gradual rejection of woodwork over time. Dominick caught Raymond up on some of things he had missed in the human world. After a while, Farrah was leaning against Dominick's leg, so he scooped her up and soon she was snoozing on his shoulder. A few more adult elves came over and joined the conversation, asking Dominick about his previous life.

There were a few pauses for more introductions and one to break up an argument between two of the younger boys. At first, Dominick was a little shocked that lectures about sharing were even a thing in the North Pole. Then, he remembered that part of the reason he was enjoying this sledding adventure so much was because it was distracting him from the fact that Jeffery was back at the cottage, getting ready for his date with a woman Dominick was quickly falling for.

Chris came back eventually, duck tucked under his arm

like she was in a time out. "Fatherhood looks good on you," he joked. Dominick let out a chuckle of his own, but he didn't feel like Chris was wrong. Farrah was still snoozing on his shoulder and Waltie had been by several times to introduce him to children who fell under Santa's banner. It all made sense to Dominick. He couldn't explain it, but it did. It felt right.

Eventually, more of the younger kids started slowing down and the elves started to herd them back to the village for dinner and bedtime. Raymond told him he was about to do the same. So they all headed back to the village and, on Farrah the Fifth's insistence, Harvey brought Dominick, Chris and Brendan to St. Nick's Pop & Slice, the North Pole's Pizza Emporium, so they could have dinner with the kids. Dominick had Chicago deep dish for the first time and listened as the kids chatted away.

After, Farrah insisted they come along for bedtime, so they all followed the caretaker elves and joined in with the bedtime North Pole edition. It went pretty fast, since the kids who didn't want a bath didn't actually need one. All they had to do was cross the threshold and poof they were bedtime ready, in thermals and footie pajamas. Just like the other buildings, the kids' quarters were strangely large on the inside, compared to how they looked on the outside.

They had a big playroom and a crafting space, a room for all kinds of games, board and video. Harvey explained they also had classrooms for the kids who wanted a semblance of school. They didn't run a full school year, but some of them were still curious about math and science, and some just liked learning random things. They ended up in what Farrah called the Cozy Room, which was packed with couches, oversized chairs and bean bags where the kids could just chill. Its roaring fireplace had no screen, which gave Dominick a temporary heart attack, but he reminded himself that everyone was safe.

The kids loved how "silly" Mr. Chris and his duck friend were, so he was deputized to read them a bedtime story. In the end, Cookie, the anthropomorphic cookie, found her friends and all was well, at Christmas time. Farrah wanted to show them where the kids slept and, again, Dominick was in awe of their quarters. A room for thousands of kids had somehow been constructed into a warm space with cool bunk beds, trundle beds and canopy beds, depending on the kid.

Dominick tucked Farrah into her bottom bunk, which was so fancy it would cost a good ten grand to build in today's human dollars, according to Raymond. He thanked her for showing them around. Across the room, Chris was busy getting in some last minute impressions with his adoring audience.

"Are we going to see you tomorrow?" Farrah asked, yawning.

"I'm not sure," Dominick replied quietly as the lights began to dim.

"I think we will," she said, before she lowered her voice even more. "I think you and Mr. Chris are here to stay."

"What about Mr. Brendan and Mr. Jeffery?" he asked, trying not to think of the "I see dead people" tone little kids loved to take, even in the happiest place on Earth.

"I haven't met Mr. Jeffery. Mr. Brendan doesn't belong here."

"Oh?" Dominick said louder than he meant to, but Farrah was done talking. She rolled over and was asleep almost immediately. Dominick stood up, too stunned to speak, and came eye to eye with Waltie, who was apparently the occupant of the top bunk. He shot Dominick a smug look and a shrug before closing his eyes too. Dominick had seen enough movies to know when to believe kids, especially when it came to the supernatural, but he still wasn't sure how to take either of their endorsements or their rejection of Brendan. From what he saw, the bear of a man had been a hit on the sledding slopes. Maybe Dominick just wasn't sure of how it would all go down.

He knew how he felt about Tiffany, but he couldn't ignore everything she'd told him or what Harvey and Shauna had shared. What if she picked Chris and asked Dominick to stay on as an elf? What if she picked Jeffery and the rest of them went off to Heaven, never to see her again? For all he knew, Jeffery was charming the pants off her at that very moment.

25

As they walked back to the village, leaving Pepper and Shadow behind with the kids, Dominick kept his mouth shut, listening as Brendan, Harvey and Chris talked. Brendan surprisingly didn't say anything weird or fucked up. Like the rest of them, he'd had a great time playing with the kids and meeting the other elves. Dominick decided the best move was to file what little Farrah had said away in the back of his mind and focus on learning more about being the best Santa for the job. If he needed to warn Tiffany, he would, but for now, he needed to mind his business and keep it pushing.

They ended the night at a pub called Kringle's. It had karaoke, so Chris was in Heaven, dominating the mic and entertaining the elves with song after song. Dominick was just happy they had actual beer that never made you drunk. Chris tried to get him on stage, but he was able to shake him off.

"If I'm gonna perform," he shouted back, "I'm doing a slow jam and Mrs. Claus better be in the audience." The elves ate that shit right up as Chris smirked back at him, shaking his head. He knew Dominick had won this round. Brendan joined him instead and by the end, half the pub—including the duck—was up there with them, screaming eighties hair metal.

Time didn't entirely matter in this place, but after a while, Harvey suggested they head back to meet Jeffery at the cottage and at least take a breather if they decided not to sleep. The three of them glanced at each other over Harvey's head before they headed to the door. They may not get anything out of him, but Jeffery's date with Tiffany could change the whole trajectory of the Santa selection process.

Harvey wished them a goodnight and left them with firm instructions to contact him if they needed anything. They piled into a shiny red Cadillac Escalade, a shade Dominick had never seen on the streets of L.A., and Franklin, the wagon driver from the hayride, drove them back up to the cottage. When they stepped inside, Jeffery was sitting by the fire, reading volume six of the *History of Giving*. He was in a dark navy suit and he'd finally ditched his City of Pittsburgh hat. He was bald—not by choice—but the look worked for him. Pepper had made her way back and was asleep at his feet.

"Hey! It's the big man, Jeffery. Looking sharp!" Chris shouted as he and Brendan danced across the house, still high from their karaoke experience.

"You three look like you had a good time," he said, closing the book. The calm confidence about him gave nothing away. Dominick joined them on the couch and waited for Jeffery to spill the beans or for Brendan to ask any overly intrusive question.

"We had a great time," Chris said, setting Quackie down. "Sledding, pizza, a thrilling bedtime story, karaoke. What a day."

"We spent the afternoon with the kids," Dominick clarified.

"Ah. Allie had a lot to say about the children. I hope I meet more of them tomorrow."

"So?" Brendan pressed, right on cue. "How'd it go with the Missus? Should we all start packing?"

"No. We had a lovely time at a restaurant that overlooks the whole village near the North Pole sign. We had a nice meal and just talked."

"And?" Brendan pressed some more, waggling his eyebrows.

Jeffery didn't respond. He just stared back at Brendan, a look of confusion and disgust spreading over his face. He might have mugged Tiffany down, but it was in poor taste to talk about it. Sufficiently shamed with a single look, Brendan flopped back in his chair with a groan.

"I'm off to bed," Jeffery said, sliding the book back on the shelf. "Christopher, Mrs. Claus said she would send a ride for you in the morning and they'll have everything you need to get ready."

"Excellent!" Chris sprung up from his seat. "Since Tiffany and I are gonna have so much sex tomorrow, I should probably get some sleep. Night, chumps." Dominick snorted as he watched Chris skip up the stairs, the duck right behind him. Jeffery followed.

With Farrah's words still heavy on his mind, Dominick considered sticking by Brendan to make sure he didn't commit interrealm crimes that would get him kicked out of the running, but Brendan was grown. If he really wanted to do or say anything that would fuck up his chances, Dominick wasn't sure he could stop him.

"I'm gonna head up," he said, just as Pepper meandered over to his side. He gave her head a scratch, lowkey grateful that she didn't pick Brendan.

"I'm gonna watch T.V. or read or something. I'm too keyed up to sleep."

"Alright. Well, I'll see you in the morning."

Brendan held out his fist for a bump, which Dominick returned before heading up to bed. Like Harvey had promised, the ornament Tiffany had picked out for him was sitting on a nest of tissue paper on the nightstand. He took the Medal of Valor out of his pocket and set it beside the ornament for safe keeping.

On the bed, were some slippers and a fresh set of pajamas. Dominick shed his snow gear and took a quick shower. Of course the water pressure was just as he liked it. He wasn't dead enough to skip the process of brushing his teeth and lotioning up. Luckily, everything he needed was in plain sight on the bathroom counter. Going commando, he changed into the pajama pants and decided to skip the button-up shirt that came with it.

Back in the bedroom, Pepper was cuddled up with a for-real skunk, asleep at the foot of the bed. Dominick had never had a pet or been pro animal on the furniture, but he wasn't sure Pepper or the skunk would listen to him. He decided to let them have this round and took a seat against the mountain of pillows.

He picked up the golden phone and pulled up his conversation with Tiffany. He imagined her in a conference room at the top of Santa's workshop with Harvey, Shauna, the Spirit of Christmas and a selection of elves, reviewing the day and ranking him and the boys on a massive leaderboard. Maybe the set up wasn't that dramatic and he wouldn't be surprised if she was busy or sleeping herself. He sent her a quick text.

I hope you had a good night.

And I hope tomorrow is less stressful for you.

He moved to set the phone on the nightstand when it rumbled in his hand. He smiled like a fool when he saw a response from Tiffany.

That's very sweet of you.

Tomorrow would be much better if I could say goodnight to you in person.

I just have to check.

Is this Tiffany?

Or Shauna trying to lure me into a horny trap?

It's Tiffany. I promise.

Go to your closet.

Dominick looked over at the closed door. He'd appreciate it if Tiffany didn't jump out and try to scare the shit out of him. Still, he went to investigate. He opened the door and light poured in. It was a portal. He looked through and saw it opened to a long hallway. Going back to his bed, he grabbed the slippers and then stepped over the magical threshold. When he glanced over his shoulder, the wall had closed up behind him and when he looked forward again, a neatly compact bouquet of red roses appeared in his hand. Clearly the magic of this place had a plan.

He sensed something to his left. Two nutcracker statues that had to be at least twenty feet tall stood at the end of the hall, guarding a large wooden door, covered in ornate carvings. It reminded him of the first door Gabriel had led him through that morning. God, what a day he'd had. Suddenly, the door opened with a pop and a creak, and Tiffany stepped out.

"He's with me, guys," she said to the nutcrackers. They fucking moved, the giant wooden statues. Dominick would have been frozen in shock if he hadn't seen what Tiffany was wearing. Red mesh short shorts with white piping and one of those football jersey type t-shirts with NORTH POLE and the number twenty-five on it, cropped so it just barely covered her breasts. Dominick felt his dick swell and his palms tingle at the sight of her. It didn't even matter that she'd put this sexy ass look together with a pair of Garfield slippers. If she let him, he was gonna spend all night worshiping her body.

"Why are you just standing there?" she practically purred. "I thought you wanted to say goodnight."

26

Tiffany tried to be subtle as she pulled in a deep breath. She knew Dominick was just a man who didn't hold any of the powers the North Pole could bestow, but peace on Earth, he looked good without a shirt on. He made his way to her, stepping between the towering guards. After the day she'd had, she was just happy to see him. But the bare chest and his broad shoulders? A simple goodnight kiss wouldn't be enough. He stopped in front of her, leaving barely an inch between the swell of her breasts and the perfectly wide, muscular body of his.

"Mrs. Claus. It's good to see you," Dominick said, the rumble in his deep voice sending a spark right to the height of her core. She felt her nipples growing harder under the fabric of her t-shirt.

"It's nice to see you too, Mr. Bell. Are these for me?" she said, trailing her finger over one of the soft rose petals.

"I'm gonna be honest. These just appeared in my hand when I walked through the wall, but if I knew where the Flower Emporium was, I would have picked them up myself."

"Sometimes, if the magic knows you want or need something, it'll give it to you. Not like a working solar system made out of carbon-free matter, that might take some work, but it can handle flowers," she explained. "It's a good sign that the North Pole likes you. You obviously needed to bring this goddess an offering."

"Well, I'm glad me and the walls are on the same page. These are for you." Dominick handed her the flowers. As she pressed the fresh blossoms to her nose, his fingers trailed over the exposed skin of her belly. Goosebumps erupted all over her skin.

"At the risk of mounting you in front of our nutcracker friends, do you want to come inside?"

Dominick tilted his head, a little smirk lifting the edge of his mustache. "Do you want me to come? Inside?"

"I will leave you out here and make you and your erection walk back to the cottage," she teased.

"We should definitely go inside then."

Tiffany grabbed his hand and led him into her home, the door closing softly behind them on its own. She gave Dominick a moment to take the space in as she brought a small vase into existence and set the flowers down on the entry table.

"What do you think? Shauna had the design elves remodel this morning."

He glanced at her, then at the flowers in their new spot, before he looked up at the high ceiling. "What's that show called? *Doctor Who*? This place is that Tardis thing. Small on the outside, huge on the inside."

"It's exactly like that," Tiffany laughed.

"What did it look like this morning?"

"Hmmm, very brown," she said looking around. "Laurence, the previous Santa, was really into rich leathers and a lot of red and gold plaid. It was beautiful, but I needed a refresh." Shauna had done just as she'd asked. A bit of French country with a holiday twist. White with blue, green and gold. Cozy, but elegant. She was very happy and she realized she hoped Dominick liked it too.

"It's nice," he replied. "You wanna show me the rest?"

"Yeah," she said, her heart warming a little more. "Come on." Together they walked down to the great room. She might have been dancing around to some Donna Summer just to reset her nerves before he'd sent that text, but now a smooth jazz version of her favorite Christmas song was softly filling the air. The twinkling lights hanging from the decorative plasterwork above were dimmed. She had a fire going and a fresh Christmas tree waiting to be dressed in the corner.

Dominick seemed drawn to the massive picture window overlooking the village, so she followed him over to take in the view. It was late, but elves were milling about, a few stragglers still enjoying the skating rinks.

"This place is pretty amazing," he said, before he turned to her. Tiffany was about to ask him how the rest of his day went, but his intense gaze trapped her voice in her throat as it traveled over her face. He reached up and lightly drew his fingers over her neck, multiplying her goosebumps. "I missed you today."

"You did?" she replied, her voice coming on a breathy sigh.

"You sound surprised."

Tiffany shrugged. "You know, busy working mom. Sometimes I get lost in the shuffle. I don't know that a Santa has ever *missed* me before."

A deep frown settled on Dominick's face. He stepped closer and wrapped his arms around her. "If it's not me, however it goes down, you deserve someone who misses you when you're not around. You deserve someone who can't get you out of their head. The next Santa better get your face tattooed on his forearm where he can see every time you're not together."

"A tattoo?!" she laughed as the tears gathered at the corners of her eyes. She couldn't stop herself from pressing her palms to his magnificent chest, which was dusted with soft hair. She needed to touch him. Everything about him was warm and strong. Something inside her needed this. Needed him. If things went her way, Dominick Bell would stay the night.

"That's the least they can do. You look out for some many people. You deserve to be a priority, not a consolation prize."

"I want it to be you," she confessed. If she lost Dominick, she knew it would hurt, but she didn't see the point of keeping it to herself. "I have something to tell you. Chris is out of the running."

"Why?" Dominick asked, clearly shocked and a little angry. "He was great with the kids today and then he charmed half the village tonight during karaoke."

"See? How can I not want it to be you? Clearly there's something here between us, something we both want, and you're still thinking of the others. That's what we need in a Santa."

"I'm not fighting it, but what happened with Chris?"

"He's going to stay and be an elf. We decided this afternoon."

"Okay, now!" Dominick replied, a genuine smile wiping that frown away. "That's good, right?"

"It's great. Just like you said, he gets on well with the other elves and when I got back from dinner, several of the kids came to find me, begging me to keep him no matter what. He wants to be here and the North Pole wants him here. It's perfect."

"I love it. Good on him."

"But! Don't say anything to the others yet. You know he's an entertainer. He wants to do a big reveal tomorrow and we'll give him his ears then." A sudden look of concern came over his features. "Hey, what's up?"

"Just deciding between whether I'm in a 'see something, say something' situation or if I should just mind my own business, but I should probably tell you if you don't know. I met Farrah the Fifth today."

"I know. I got a very solid report on her behalf from the caretaker elves."

"Well then, you might know this too. She told me that Chris and I were going to stay. She had no opinion on Jeffery, but she did say something pretty specific about Brendan. She said he doesn't belong here. Kinda brutal, but I guess that's how little kids do things."

It was Tiffany's turn to frown. She wasn't wild about the way Brendan had acted when they were picking out ornaments, but she didn't think it was disqualifying. The children loved him and the Spirit hadn't counted him in out yet. She'd just have to wait and see.

"I'm glad you told me. I'll keep an eye on him tomorrow.

Gabriel is very careful about who they pick, but we are all still creatures of choice. Maybe he's just going through some stuff or maybe he's changing his mind."

"I don't remember dying, but being poisoned sounds pretty fucked up. He could still be working through that."

"Yeah... but thank you. How was the rest of your day?" Tiffany asked, taking his hand. She led him to one of the comfy armchairs that were wide enough for two and once he sat down, she didn't waste a moment crawling into his lap. It was the perfect spot for them to enjoy the fire.

"It was a good day. The kids are pretty funny. And fearless," Dominick shifted her weight and pulled her closer as he told her about their trip to the post office and their sledding adventure. She should have been shocked by how easy it was to be with him this way, but it felt so natural. She felt like she belonged with him and that warm tug in her chest confirmed it.

"They're such a big part of what makes this place special. Their energy, their joy. It wouldn't be the same without them running around."

"I can definitely see that now. Though, I do wish the little ones would stop with the ominous messages."

"It's how they keep you on your toes," she laughed.

"Waltie could stare right through a man's soul. Anyway, how was your date with Jeffery?" His tone held no jealousy, which she appreciated.

"It was interesting," she said honestly. "He's very thorough. He asked me a lot of logistical questions, which was good, but it was difficult to get through."

"Difficult how?" Dominick asked. Like he knew what she would say next, he drew his confident fingers up her thigh and began toying with the hem of her shorts. She couldn't help the way her legs pinched together, making the ache she'd been feeling between them since the moment he'd arrived that much worse. Seconds later, she feel could his erection rising against her hip.

"I was kind of distracted. Earlier today, this extremely handsome man kissed me and then he smacked me on my ass, and I haven't stopped thinking about him since."

"Oh. I can see how that would make things hard. Are you still feeling distracted? Is there anything I could help you with now?"

Tiffany sat up and moved, so she was straddling his lap. She knew if her gaze left his dark brown eyes that were blazing in the fire light, she'd see his erection pressing against the fabric of his pants. She also knew that if his gaze slipped any lower than where it was now on her lips, he'd see how hard her nipples were. And any lower than that, he'd spot the arousal coating the tops of her thighs. His hands rested lightly on her hips, but it wasn't enough.

"I think things would be a lot better if you touched me."

27

"Mrs. Claus, are you about to use me for my body?" Dominick asked.

Tiffany's tongue darted out and wet her bottom lip before she nodded. She'd thought about the years it had taken Laury to know her well and figure out what she liked, and she had a feeling it wouldn't take Dominick long at all. He sat up and leaned closer, wrapping his hands around her waist. "You want my hands or my mouth first?" he asked, his voice a low rumble.

Before Tiffany could tell him she wanted both, she wanted all of him, his hands were already circling the curves of her body. One hand eased down her overheating skin and took a firm hold of her ass. His other hand moved under the swell of her breast and further up, moving the fabric of her cropped t-shirt out of the way. She felt a soft gasp leave her mouth as he dipped his head and drew his tongue over her puckering nipple. Tiffany's fingers lightly scratched at the back of his head, holding him close as he sucked and licked at her. Her hips flexed forward, chasing the friction and the penetration she desperately wanted.

"It would be pretty cruel for me to make you wait, huh?" Dominick said.

Tiffany nodded again, too scared of her own voice because she knew all that would come out was a lot of begging.

"Well, let's see what we can do." The hand on her ass moved around to her front and between her thick thighs, pushing the damp patch of fabric aside. Her breath hitched as the knuckle on his forefinger brushed over her clit. He did it again and again, until he shifted his whole hand and pressed two strong fingers through her soaking lips. "Goddamn, you are so wet. Is this all for me?" he asked before he switched over to her neglected nipple, gently biting down.

"Yes," Tiffany moaned. "Please don't stop."

"Why would I do that?" He added another finger and slowly pressed inside. Tiffany couldn't stop her hips from moving, riding his hand as more moans and desperate whimpers left her mouth. A moment later, his fingers were gone and her eyes snapped open, almost in anger that he would betray her that way. She was about to argue or beg as she watched him lift his hand to his lips and lick his fingers clean. Tiffany almost fainted at the sound of his groan. "Fuck, you taste good."

His hand went right back to work, rubbing and then pressing so deep that she knew she wouldn't last much longer. His other hand gripped the back of her neck and he held her close as he captured her lips in a deep, perfect kiss. Her hips really started moving then, mimicking the absolutely filth way his tongue was moving inside her mouth. She had to pull back, gritting her teeth as she pressed her forehead to his. An orgasm rocked through her. She cried out, trembling in his grasp. It wasn't enough. She wanted more and she was ready to beg for it.

Suddenly, Dominick looped his arm around her waist and stood effortlessly. "Where's your bedroom?" he asked.

"The door on the left, right behind you," she breathed, entranced by the look of determination on his face. With his long stride, he had them at the foot of her new bed in no time. Setting her gently on top of her fresh quilt, he shucked off his pants and gave her soaked shorts the same treatment.

"Do I need protection?" he asked, glancing at her bedside table. "Do you have any?"

"We don't need it. No pregnancies or infections here in the North Pole, but thank you for asking. Come here." She held her hands out for him, but he just looked back at her, his gaze roaming every inch of her body. She closed her legs, not to hide her core, but just to show off the voluptuous curves of her thigh and her ass. Dominick smiled.

"Do you know how beautiful you are? How fucking sexy you are?"

"I have an idea, but I don't mind being adored."

"Worshipped." Dominick climbed over her, his hardened dick jutting out from his hips. The length of him was perfectly long and thick. She couldn't wait to feel him moving inside her. Gently, he took hold of her knee and opened her legs again. He leaned down and brushed his lips to hers. "You deserve to be worshipped, Mrs. Claus."

"Then worship me, Mr. Bell."

He didn't have a witty comeback or another seductive remark. Instead, the smooth crown of his erection pressed against her aching entrance. Tiffany shifted her hips, making it easier for him to slide home.

"I knew it," Dominick breathed against her lips. He pulled back, just a little, before he pressed deep again, nice and slow. Tiffany dug her nails into the soft skin of his back. He let out a low hiss and flexed his hips, pumping in and out, in an ideal rhythm.

"You knew what, baby?" she whispered back.

"I knew it would be this good. I knew being with you like this would feel right." He pressed into her, thrusting deeper and harder, but not faster. For a split second she thought about how it had taken her months to get Laurence to understand that subtle, but very clear difference. In the next second, the only person she could think about was Dominick. He took her so well, made love to her in a way that left her craving more even after the second and third orgasms rocked through her.

She reached up, gripping the quilt in her hands, grinding herself down on his amazing body, her pussy gripping his dick with every roll of her hips. She thought maybe she would be satisfied. She came two more times before Dominick's own jaw clenched and he trembled above her, filling her with every drop.

He rolled off and held her close as they made their way under the covers. Tiffany nuzzled against his chest, feeling well worn out and strangely complete as he drew lazy circles on her arm. She looked up at him and his eyes were focused on the ceiling. He tilted his chin up, motioning to the single sprig of mistletoe hanging above the bed.

"How come those aren't all over the North Pole?"

"For like a month, we had them up in every doorway and

the elves were just using it as an excuse to make out, so they are only in a few places."

"That's a good spot." He leaned down and pressed a soft kiss to her lips. "How do I keep you, Mrs. Claus? I'm not ready to let you go."

Tiffany swallowed, fighting back the tears. So much had changed in such a short time. Dominick meant something to her and she didn't want to let him go either, but that didn't change the fact that it wasn't her decision to make. She'd been telling the truth when she'd said that she'd been thinking about him all through dinner and that she wanted to feel him close to her.

She'd just left out the fact that it was slowly becoming clear that Jeffery was an excellent candidate for Santa. He needed to spend time with the children, but Allie and Jessica loved him and she definitely couldn't count out Dasher's initial thoughts. The choice simply wasn't hers and no matter how badly she wanted him, there was a chance that Dominick wouldn't be here in two days.

Could she ask him to stay on as an elf? Maybe. Would that be smart or fair to either of them? Absolutely not. So, maybe all they had was tonight and she refused to let that go by with any ounce of regret.

Tiffany rolled up on her elbow and took in every inch of Dominick's handsome face. Love was growing between them and she knew neither of them could deny it.

"If it was up to me, I'd choose you. I need you to know that."

"Okay." Dominick nodded before he leaned down and kissed her again, making it knowing that he'd received the message loud and clear.

28

Dominick had fucked up. He knew the rules and the stakes, and still, he had gone and fallen for Tiffany. He hoped like hell that he would be the last man standing, but what if there was just something that made Jeffery or Brendan a better choice for the job of Santa? He felt too much for Tiffany to even think about either of them loving her the way he wanted to. But he couldn't deny what she was trying to tell him. This was one involved-ass process and when so much was weighing on the outcome, so many people? Maybe the way things felt when it was just the two of them wouldn't be enough for them to make it together.

They came together one more time, finding each other in her sheets, before Tiffany used her magic to bring them some midnight snacks. She sat across from him now, in a fluffy plaid robe, her legs tucked under her as she nibbled on a piece of apricot. He appreciated every inch of her naked body, but she looked cute as hell all bundled up, her hair mushed in the back. Most importantly, she looked happy.

"Tell me more about what the day to day is like," he asked her. He took another sip of the apple butterscotch drink she'd conjured up for him.

"So basically, I handle the elves and all the goings on here at the North Pole and you—Santa—spend most of the year selecting which people you want to appear to in person, practicing the flight pattern with the reindeer, confirming with NORAD and the other international aerospace commissions so you and the sleigh don't get shot at."

"Wait, so there are humans that know Santa exists for sure?" he asked, reaching for another espresso cookie.

"Yes, but we're talking about the kinds of government employees who've lost all sense of whimsy. To them, Santa's just another pilot."

"That's a shame."

"But, yeah, I keep things running smoothly here so Santa can keep things running smoothly out there."

"So really, this is your world and we're just living in it."

"Basically," Tiffany laughed. "This is the most downtime I'll have until the day after Christmas. Once we pick a new Santa, he needs to immediately get with the Spirit of Christmas and get training underway."

Dominick nodded. He could handle that. He liked working. He liked to keep busy. He liked learning new things and he knew the North Pole had a lot to teach him.

"Can I ask you something? It's not a small thing, but I'm just trying to get to know you more," he said. He didn't want to upset her. Their time together was just ticking away and if he could ask, he knew he should.

"Yeah, what's up?"

"Do you remember how you passed away?"

Tiffany's eyes widened for a split second before she covered her mouth and snorted. "Yeah, I do. It's kind of ironic sitting here talking to a firefighter. I died in a fire."

"Oh god," Dominick groaned, falling back against the headboard.

"Yeah. Nothing as calm and easy as being t-boned by a speeding Honda. I guess I'll tell you the whole story, but first, I need to repeat that I want to be here. I love living in the North Pole. I love working with the elves and making my Santa my bitch."

"Okay," Dominick laughed in return. "Tell me."

"So I was born a free person in New Hampshire."

"No idea where that is."

"In those times it was about a three days ride to Boston. If traffic is with you now, take 93 North for about forty-five minutes and you're there."

Dominick tried to picture what he remembered of the east coast and the interstates. And all the NFL stadiums. "So like an hour north of Foxborough?"

"Yes! Trust me, you'll know where *everything* is if you get the gig. Anyway, we lived in this small town on the Squamscott River. It was a shipping hub of sorts. My great-grandfather was taken from Benin by a ship captain when he was nine and brought over, but he was freed when he was twenty-five. He ran the local stables and my father took over for him. My mother was a seamstress. She showed me how to make dolls and teddy bears from the leftover scraps and I started selling them in town.

Dominick tried to picture it, her childhood on the water.

"She taught me how to quilt too," she said, pointing to the giant tapestry hanging on the far wall. Dominick had noticed it, of course, but he'd been a little too preoccupied to comment on the decor. The quilt was almost the size of the whole wall. With a patchwork design, she'd created an image of a bright star shining over Santa's village.

"You made that?" he said in awe.

"Yup," she smiled back. "I don't make toys any more, but I love quilting and any kind of needle work."

"That's amazing. Sorry, go on."

"When I was sixteen, my father was traveling down to Boston to check out some horses. He brought my brother and me along so I could sell a few dolls, but we never made it. All three of us were kidnapped on the road and sold."

"Tiff—" She held up her hand to stop whatever apology he would offer.

"Everyone who had a hand in it is not enjoying their afterlife. Trust me. We were separated and I ended up in Virginia. I was forced to work for three different families. The last plantation I was at, the mistress of the house wanted the very best for her daughter and thought it would be *just* the best if she had her own toy maker on call. I made almost all their dresses, but the toys were her little party trick.

"The day I died, I was on the back porch, showing her daughter how to attach the arms and the head to a teddy bear, when I heard her mother screaming. Others came running, but I was the first one inside. Back then, the clothing women wore was different. More layers, a lot more fabric, more combustible."

"I think I know where this is going."

"Oh no, it's worse than you think. She was on fire. Her left side and her back. When I came into the room, she stopped screaming for half a second and stared right at me.

She cursed me, saying it was my fault because I made the dress. She tackled me and rolled us back toward the fireplace. So we're both on fire and her dress caught a chair and the curtains when she went after me. The whole room was up before they could get to us. When I woke up, I was sitting by the Squamscott River speaking to Gabriel."

"Hmmm," Dominick replied. "What did he say to you?"

"He told me how much I'd loved the winters as a little girl and how much I'd loved the holiday celebrations. The other free Black people in town had thrown get togethers. Some of the local enslaved people were allowed to come. It was special. He asked me if I wanted to help grow and spread that kind of joy. The rest of my family was still alive so no one was waiting for me. So I said yes, if it meant I could leave whenever I wanted."

"And you're still here."

"I am. The first Santa, Joseph, he was kind, but we were more like acquaintances. I wasn't officially Mrs. Claus until about three years before he left. I was more like the head elf up until that point, compared to how it is now. Our second Santa, Theodore, he was... I'll be real, okay?"

"Okay," Dominick laughed.

"The man was horny as heck, but it worked out. I knew things from when I was alive, against my will, unfortunately. But he figured he had certain liberties, since I was technically his wife. I told him I was open to it, but I had questions about sex and how it worked when it was consensual. That was music to his ears. Again, no love there, but we had fun and the way we got along seemed to boost morale even more around here. The elves really started to look at us as a couple."

"And the last Santa?"

"My best friend," she said with a warm smile. "And it wasn't anything like the way I feel with you."

Dominick sat up and, like she'd read his mind, Tiffany used her magic to move their snack party off the bed and onto a fancy wooden cart right beside it. She moved to her knees and shuffled closer until she was back in his arms. He had to accept that there was no concept of time anymore, or that maybe all of time existed all at once. He felt like he'd already loved her in the past and they had this whole future waiting for them. He wasn't sure how any of that worked, but maybe in the morning he'd track down Essee and do some serious begging.

"I didn't have any children, but my brother and sisters did, so I have relatives that are still around. They are loved and the angels look out for them," she said, letting out a deep sigh as she picked up his hand and started tracing the lines of his palm with her fingertips. "A cookie for your thoughts?" She glanced up at him before she turned her attention back to his hand.

"What am I not thinking about?"

They both shook a little when she giggled. "It's your turn to tell me your whole life story. All the details that weren't in your file."

"That's what I was thinking about. I was lucky enough that I wasn't in any foster situations that were straight up physically abusive, but I spent my whole childhood trying to be quiet and invisible. My whole goal was just to grow up. And then when I realized I could drive a fire engine as my job, I just focused on that."

Dominick thought back to the community college job fair

he'd gone to with his foster brother and how he learned about how to get his CDL. "I talked to some teamsters about driving trucks for movies, but being a firefighter just sounded more—"

"Exciting?"

"Yeah."

"Was it?"

"Sometimes," Dominick chuckled. "A lot more car accidents than I'd anticipated at fifteen, but it's definitely never dull and, unlike the cops, we actually help people in emergencies. Even when it wasn't actually an emergency, I liked showing up for people. I liked feeling useful instead of trying to blend into a wall so I wouldn't get kicked out."

"That must have been hard. You found your parents though, right?"

Damn. Everything was in that file. "Yeah. My mom was really young when she had me. She lived over on the East side. My dad was one of her grandmother's neighbors. I look exactly like him. One of his buddies knew my last foster dad. He did some asking around and connected some dots, but I was seventeen then and neither of them were exactly warm fuzzy people, so I just kept it moving. Eventually, Station 94 became home."

"I don't know if it will help any, but your fellow firefighters? They loved you a lot. You were the heart of that place, the level head and the calm in the storm. It's why Gabriel and Jubilee picked you. You're a good man, Dominick, and you are loved."

Tears slipped down his cheeks. He was able to dash a few away before Tiffany leaned up and kissed him. He kissed her back and, a few seconds later, all that hurt and loss was gone.

Dominick slipped his hands under her robe, feeling his way across her warm, soft skin. She moved again to straddle his lap, shrugging the fluffy fabric off her shoulders so there was nothing between them. Arching up on her knees, she drew her slick clit up and down the length of his hard dick. Dominick gripped her ass and held her close. He looked up at her before drawing a wet streak between her tits with his tongue.

Tiffany bit her lip, her gaze darkening as she looked back at him. She flexed her hips again and again, painting herself with his precum. "I know it is completely impossible for you to get me pregnant, but..."

"But?" he asked, his eyebrow arching up. Tiffany reached between her legs and put him inside of her warm, sweet pussy.

"We can have some fun trying." Her teasing lasted long enough for Dominick to thrust all the way home. Tiffany let out the sexiest fucking noises as she wrapped her arms around him and starting working her hips with some true effort. As he lightly gripped the side of her neck and captured her lips, he knew begging wasn't the way to go with Essee or the elves. He would tell all of them, Dasher, Rudolph and their homegirls too, that Tiffany was his and he belonged to Tiffany. He wasn't walking away without a fight.

29

When Dominick opened his eyes the next morning, he was pleasantly surprised to find Tiffany practically suctioned to his back. He'd shared his bed plenty of times, but he'd never woken up as the little spoon. He patted Tiffany's hand and started to roll over when she gripped him tighter and let out an adorable moan.

"No. You're so warm," she said, pressing soft kisses to his back. Dominick laughed at the pathetic moan that was threatening to leave his own mouth.

"The front of me is warm too. Come here." Dominick rolled out of her grasp, then quickly pulled her on top of him. Tiffany squirmed so her head was resting perfectly on his chest and his rising erection was exactly where it needed to be, right between her thighs.

They hadn't gotten much sleep. They'd spent most of the night talking and when they weren't talking, they were coming up with new and interesting ways to come together.

He'd spent a nice amount of time with his head between her legs, licking, sucking, worshipping her like he ought to. She'd done the same and while Dominick had loved the way her mouth felt sliding up and down his dick, a lovesick part of his heart had felt like she was too far away. She'd tried to make him finish inside her mouth twice and each time he'd pulled her up so he could kiss her and bury himself deep inside her instead.

Tiffany had a little freak in her, which Dominick absolutely loved, but he also realized he couldn't get enough of just holding her in his arms. She looked up at him with those big brown eyes and Dominick wondered if they could get away with ditching the fellas all day. The answer was no.

"I have bad news," Tiffany said, her lower lip jutting out.

"What? It would look bad if we ran off and got married this morning?" he joked, kinda.

He couldn't stop touching her. Fingers trailing down her soft shoulder, his other hand tracing the shell of her delicately pointed ear. His magical girl. "I actually think Shauna would cover for us, but no, Pepper is outside waiting to bring you back."

"I can't just walk back through the wall?"

"You could, but the guys are up and about ten minutes ago, Brendan went looking for you."

"So they know I'm not in the house. Damn, alright."

Tiffany reached up and touched his beard. "I have to have a quick meeting with a few elves and I need to meet with Chris. After he gets his ears, I'll make some time for you and Brendan. And then maybe you can come visit me tonight?"

Dominick nodded. Of course he would, but Dominick knew what she wasn't saying. Their time was running out.

Sometime in the next thirty-six hours, the North Pole would choose a Santa. "I'll ask the wall to give me different flowers and maybe some chocolates this time."

"That's so romantic," she said with a grin. "I'll see you in a few hours?"

"Yeah, okay," he grumbled. Tiffany rolled off him with an adorable laugh and trotted to the bathroom. Dominick sat on the edge of the bed, mustering the energy to leave her, when a pile of clothes appeared beside him. He smiled as he saw the Dodgers jacket folded on the bottom. He stretched out of habit and realized he felt better than he had in all his living days. Quickly, he slipped on the boxer briefs, chinos and t-shirt, before he pulled on the fresh pair of socks and new black boots. Just as he put on the jacket, Tiffany walked back into the bedroom in all her Mrs. Claus glory.

She walked over to him in a short, red velvet dress with white fur on the bottom and on the cuffs of her wrists. She had a traditional Santa hat on that looked very expensive and a different pair of white fur boots with intricate stitching up the sides. Makeup done, hair fresh. She looked amazing.

She adjusted the collar of his jacket and pressed a kiss to his cheek.

"I'll see you soon. And remember, don't breathe a word to the other men about Chris. We have a little surprise planned."

"Everyone's secret is safe with me."

"Good. Now, get out," she chuckled, but Dominick had something serious he needed her to know.

"Tiffany," he said, her name on his tongue like a vow.

"Yes?"

"I'll be your Santa. I know people say things in the dark

when no clothes are involved, but I need to be clear. I want all of this and I want you."

Tiffany nodded, swallowing a thick knot in her throat. "I'll tell them."

Dominick cupped her cheeks in his hands as he leaned down to kiss her one more time before he headed back to the great room. Sure enough, Pepper was sitting at attention right by the front door.

"You ready, girl?" he asked. Pepper barked back. Dominick wanted to be Santa for the obvious reasons, but he also wanted to understand what the animals were saying.

"That's a yes," Tiffany laughed.

"I figured. It would be a shame if she was cussing me out." Dominick kissed Tiffany one more time. He couldn't help himself. Then he and the dog headed out the door.

The nutcrackers parted their sabers to let them through. Pepper continued on to another emergency exit that Dominick was positive hadn't been there the night before. It opened behind Santa's workshop, the snowy path ahead leading straight into the woods. Dominick let Pepper lead the way through the trees. He expected a portal or something to open in the next fifty feet or so, but the further they went, the trees kept getting thicker. Pepper stopped suddenly, sniffing the air. She lowered herself on all fours, bracing for attack with a low growl rumbling in her throat. He couldn't see anything but trees and snow, but clearly something was there.

"Shit," Dominick whispered to himself. He turned around, looking to run back toward the workshop, but the path behind him was gone and the trees had closed in. A second later, Dominick caught a whiff of an oddly familiar smell, something like burning flesh and sulfur. Black smoke began to billow between his feet as Pepper started going apeshit, barking like crazy. Dominick stumbled back a few steps and his shoulder slammed into a tree as Krampus appeared out of the thick dark air.

30

Pepper froze. Like, completely froze. No barking, no movement.

"Don't worry," Krampus hissed. "Your companion is just fine." Dominick quickly ducked to his right, but the trees closed in tighter, creating a solid wall of trunks, needles and branches. He was trapped. Pulling a deep breath, which unfortunately still smelled like burnt flesh, he sized the demon up as he clenched his fists. He might not be the winner, but Dominick would take a piece out of the motherfucker on his way down.

Krampus—Karl, his name was Karl—stalked closer, his big hooves stomping in the snow until barely an inch separated them.

"What do you want?" Dominick demanded, putting some extra bass in his voice.

"So testy, you humans. So easily frightened, you city dwellers. You've never come across a harmless creature like me in the forest."

"Yeah, that doesn't answer my question. What do you want?"

Karl didn't respond. He just moved in closer, his hot, rank breath wafting over Dominick's face. Dominick whipped his head away, which was a big mistake. He felt Karl's forked tongue briefly sweep along his neck just as his spiked tail wrapped around Dominick's ankle. The bile rose in Dominick's throat. He was taught to fight fair, but if he had to kick Karl in the dick, he'd do it.

"Back the fuck up," Dominick said.

"Oooh," Karl moaned, his voice vibrating in a way that made his skin crawl. "You've already laid claim to the princess, I see. I can smell her on you. You must tell me, Dominick Bell. How does she taste?"

Dominick had never had a rage blackout before, but there was a first time for everything. The thought of Karl going anywhere near Tiffany again—

"Oh?" Karl said, his whole body stilled. "Be careful with that thing."

Dominick blinked and looked at the Halligan bar that had appeared in his hand. It wasn't at the ideal angle for bashing Karl in the skull, but the poker was jabbing right into the base of his hairy throat. Dominick could hear Tiffany in his head, reminding him of the magic of this place. Sometimes it gave you exactly what you needed.

"My my, Mr. Bell. Who knew you came with sharp toys?"

"I'm going to tell you one more time and then we'll see what demon blood looks like. Back. The fuck. Up."

Karl let out an annoyed sigh and took a few large steps back, unwinding his tail from Dominick's leg. He made a show of dusting off his shoulders before he smiled, revealing two rows of sharp yellow teeth. "Will you relax?"

"Why would I do that?"

"Because I'm not here to hurt you. Here. Have your dog back." Karl flicked his tail at the air around Pepper. She came back to life and straightened her body, looking up at Karl with a mean side eye like she was cussing him out before trotting over to Dominic's side. "Though, it would be fun, I have to meet with all of the prospective Santas, since we'll be working so close together and to give you some additional options."

Dominick's palm was starting to sweat around the handle of the pry bar. "Get to the point."

"I want to offer you a job. There's a thirty-three—I mean, a twenty-five—percent chance you'll become Santa. But if you don't, there's always room for you at Krampus Corp."

Dominick didn't think it mattered that Karl knew Chris was out of the running. It wasn't something they needed to discuss and neither was his so-called job offer. This conversation was over.

"I'm good. Anything else or can you go back to wherever the hell you came from?"

"God, you're no fun. Yeah, that's all I wanted and since you've rejected me, I'm required to leave. If you do become Mr. Saint-Nicholas, I suppose I'll see you again for our annual meeting to go over the naughty list."

Fuck. Dominick realized he was actually going to have to work with this motherfucker. "Can't wait."

"Neither can I, but before I go..." Karl's thick eyebrows arched up. "Please tell me what she tastes like."

Dominick knew it was a bad idea to toss his only weapon, but he heaved that pry bar right at Karl's head as hard as he could. Right as it split his demon skin, Karl disappeared, leaving a dark cloud and his echoing cackle in his wake.

❄

Dominick was still pissed as he and Pepper made it back up the front steps of the cottage. He calmed down a little when he opened the door and was greeted with the scent of bacon. Jeffery was back at the table, surrounded by a new stack of books. Pepper ran over to him and stretched out by his feet. Brendan was in the kitchen making breakfast.

"Hey! Look who's back? Where you been?" he asked, right as Chris came skipping down the stairs.

"It's Dominick. Hey." Chris stopped short as he stepped into the kitchen, a frown hitting his face as he looked Dominick up and down. "Hey, you okay?"

"Yeah. I couldn't sleep and I went out for one of those long thinking walks. I ran into that Krampus dude Karl on the way back.

"Jesus! You know he showed up at the foot of my bed last night? I almost pooed my pantaloons," Chris replied, making Dominick laugh. Running into a demon in the woods was fucked up enough, but having him show up in a dark room while you're sleep? Hell nah.

"He found me right before my dinner with Tiffany," Jeffery added. "He asked me if I wanted to come work with him. Apparently they run a year-round torture kink cartel for adults and then scare the living daylights out of a few naughty children around the holidays. Didn't sound that appealing to me."

"Huh," Dominick replied. "He offered me a job too, but I didn't ask any follow-up questions."

"You know me. I like to know things."

"True."

"Did he run up on you?" Dominick asked Brendan. Was Krampus the reason Farrah was decidedly not Team Brendan?

Brendan nodded. "Yeah. He woke me up this morning, but I told him I was just fine where I am. It was a quick conversation. I just wish I'd had pants on."

"Hmmm," was all Dominick could say. He didn't want to picture that interaction.

"Well!" Chris declared. "Brendan, that breakfast smells amazing, but I need to go have so much day sex with Tiffany, followed by brunch."

"You could stand to be a little bit more respectful," Jeffery said. Chris walked over and pressed a wet kiss to Jeffery's bald head.

"You're right. You're still my number one. I'll be a new, well-behaved man when I return. Goodbye!" Chris swept to the front door, closing it behind him with a flourish.

"You want any of this?" Brendan asked, waving his spatula at the rising stack of bacon accumulating next to the stove.

"Yeah. Thanks." Dominick shucked off his jacket and joined Jeffery and his stack of books at the table. He needed a distraction from his racing thoughts of the night he spent in Tiffany's bed, Karl's foul breath and the new man Chris was actually about to become. They were down to three now. He didn't know how the next couple days would go, but he was more determined than ever to make it to the end, even if it only meant he could spend the rest of eternity standing between Tiffany and that bum-ass motherfucker, Karl.

31

Tiffany stood in front of the fireplace in the elves' Welcome Center. Chris's big debut would begin shortly. The news had already circulated amongst the citizens of the North Pole and they were excited to bring him into the fold. Tiffany was so glad everything had worked out where he was concerned, but she couldn't stop thinking about Dominick.

Last night had meant so much to her. More than she'd ever admit. She couldn't wait to see him again, but she was dreading the very real possibility that she would lose him soon. She looked around the room. The Spirit, Dasher, Shauna and Lee-Ann, the head caretaker elf, were all listening as Harvey gave them a recap of how the official Santa search was going. This was standard procedure and with Chris's decision to become an elf, Tiffany wasn't participating in the process.

"I think we are left with three excellent candidates," he said with a bright smile. "I'd like to hear each of your thoughts or the thoughts of your people before we move on with Christopher's celebration."

"The animal members of the North Pole community continue to put our support behind Mr. Jeffery Jefferson," Dasher expressed.

With a nod, Lee-Ann added, "As of right now, the children are in support of Mr. Brendan Kiffen. Though, that is because Christopher has decided to stay on in a different role."

"The elves reported the same to me this morning," Shauna said. "Chris was their top choice, but they are putting their support behind Brendan now. He really won them over last night during karaoke."

"I'm so sad I missed it," Tiffany laughed.

"Well, I'm sure Chris will give you an encore performance anytime."

The room grew quiet and still as they waited for the Spirit of Christmas to share her thoughts. Essee moved through the air around Dasher's antlers and came to rest on Lee-Ann's shoulder. She focused all of her energy on Tiffany, who could feel it in her heart like a penetrating laser.

"A decision has already been made," the Spirit expressed. "All that remains are the details of the journey." The silence in the room seemed to grow thicker, despite the crackle of the fire. There was no point in asking her to clarify. Essee was unlike the other creatures in The North Pole because she existed in and outside of time. If Santa had already been chosen in the future as a result of the last twenty-fours, Tiffany should see that as a good sign, because they would be in big trouble if none of the men worked out. Instead, Tiffany felt her palms starting to sweat and a sour feeling settled in her stomach.

It was one thing when her thoughts were clouded by her own uncertainties and doubts, but Essee's certainty gave her hope and absolutely terrified her in equal measure. Tiffany feigned relief and plastered a smile on her face, even though Essee could see right through her.

"That brings me comfort," she lied. "I think we would all be happy to have any one of them."

Harvey cleared his throat. "Mrs. Claus, is there anything more *you* would like to add about our candidates? Any personal thoughts?"

"Oh. Um, not particularly. I think I'll know more by the end of the day. I will definitely let you know if I have anything to share," Tiffany said. She caught the way Shauna rolled her eyes, but kept her opinions to herself.

"Well, if there's nothing more, we have a party to attend." Everyone thanked Harvey and started heading back toward the village square. Shauna stopped Tiffany with a hand on her arm.

"Mrs. Claus. May I speak to you for a moment?" she said, laying the sarcasm on extra thick.

"Of course," Tiffany said, giving her the attitude right back as Shauna tugged her over to the mantel. "What?"

"Don't 'what' me. Why didn't you put in your vote for Dominick?"

"You heard Essee. The decision has been made. There's nothing I can say that'll change that."

"Oh, that's bullshit and you know it."

"Shauna Chantal, such language," Tiffany gasped.

"Look, bitch. I know he stayed over last night and there is no way there was not some x-rated activity going on."

"Who told you?" Someone must have seen him leaving that morning.

"Mrs. Skunk was in the visitors' cottage. She saw the little Narnia stunt you pulled with his closet. You know she can't keep her mouth shut."

"Dang it."

"Yeah, dang it," Shauna said. "You asked Chris if he wanted to be an elf. Why can't you just tell everyone that you want Dominick to be your Santa?"

"Shauna, I love you, but you have to drop it. The decision's been made. Let's just enjoy the next few hours and do what Essee said, see how the details play out."

Shauna let out a huffing breath, biting her lower lip between her teeth.

"I get what you want me to do or say, but you have to drop this. I'm stressed out enough. You coming at me like this isn't helping. I know I'll be fine if it's not Dominick. I'll recover. But the more I get my hopes up, the more crushing the blow will be if it's not him. So please, let it go. I just want to enjoy today."

"Fine. I'm going behind your back and telling the others that Dominick is your man, but I won't bring it up to *you* again."

"Great. Thanks. Also, why are you even thinking about me right now? There's a new elf joining our ranks and he liiii-ikes you."

Shauna cupped her cheeks, miserably failing to hide her embarrassment. "I know. We only got a few minutes to talk this morning, but we're going to go on a little date tonight after Lee-Ann gets through a bit of his orientation."

"See, I love that for you. Don't worry about me. In a day or so, I'll be happily remarried and we can forget any of this ever happened."

"Mhmmm, yes. We will all forget this monumental shift for you and all of the North Pole. Poof! Gone."

"Right. Well, if you're done mocking me and this impossible situation I'm in, I'm off to introduce your new boyfriend, who was handpicked by the angels."

Shauna's expression dropped and she pulled Tiffany into a tight hug. "I'm sorry. I just want you to get the man that *you* want."

Tiffany squeezed her back for a few long moments before she stepped out of Shauna's grasp. "It'll all work out. Okay?" she said, giving Shauna's dimpled cheek a gentle pinch. That seemed to get her to relax.

"Yeah, okay. But can you at least do me one favor? Please tell me Dominick is good in bed. I need to know that you got one night of good dicking in all this chaos."

Tiffany let out a sputtering laugh. "The sweet, tender lovemaking befitting your elven queen was wonderful. I'll never forget it."

"Okay. Well, that's nice."

"And so was the nasty dicking that came after."

"Yesss! Atta girl."

Tiffany gave Shauna a light shove toward the door as she laughed. "Let's go."

32

Dominick could feel the energy bouncing around the village square in his bones. Through breakfast, he'd kept his word to Tiffany and not mentioned a word about Chris's new role, but he hadn't expected the big reveal to be anything like this. Harvey had shown up with a train of snowmobiles and led them back into town. They made their way to some pretty swanky, VIP seating in front of a large circular stage that was held up by log-sized candy cane supports. Motown Christmas classics pumped through the air as the elves, children and animals started filling in the space around the stage. Soon, the village center was packed.

"So, is this like a regular Tuesday?" Brendan asked Harvey over the din of the crowd.

"No," Harvey chuckled. "We welcome all the new elves differently. This one likes to make an entrance."

"Oh. Where's Chris? This seems like it would be his thing."

"He'll be along with Tiffany shortly. We wouldn't let him miss the show."

A few moments later, the music stopped and a loud, booming voice filled the air. "Citizens of the North Pole, young and old, furry and feathered, please welcome our amazing queen, your Mrs. Claus!"

The crowd went wild, cheering even louder as Tiffany appeared at the center of the stage in a cloud full of glitter, snowflakes and smoke. She was in the same short, long-sleeved dress she's been in before, but now the red velvet was covered in red sequins, making her body sparkle with every movement. She didn't appear to be mic'd up, but clearly she didn't need it because her voice carried smoothly through the air.

"Hello, my darlings!" More cheering, more applause. Dominick looked up at her, a strange pride swelling in his chest. He'd heard that old adage, something about not counting hatching chickens prematurely, but he couldn't help the way he felt. That was his woman up there, looking like a ten and addressing her people. She made her way over to their side of the stage and winked at them as she went on.

"I know there has been a lot of excitement the last couple of days. We said a farewell, which we all know is hard. I have to thank you all for being so kind and welcoming to our new guests. I promise we will have a perfect Santa soon, ready to get us right back on track for the holiday season, which is rapidly approaching. But today, a bit sooner than I'd anticipated, I think it's time for a fresh and fun hello. I'm not sure I'm the right person to do this introduction, though, so maybe I should hand things over."

With a mischievous smile, Tiffany floated off the edge of

the stage. The crowd parted as she made her way over, nestling her perfect curves between Dominick and Brendan. Dominick leaned down and kissed the edge of her pointed ear as the opening notes of "Sleigh Ride" rang out.

"That was quite the entrance, Mrs. Claus," he said.

"Just you wait," she giggled back.

"Where's Chris?" Brendan asked as the music grew louder.

"He's here. Don't worry, he's not missing a thing."

Dominick felt a little shitty as he watched Brendan look around for Chris, but not five seconds later, a flurry of smoke, fireworks and glitter erupted onstage. It was an absolute fire hazard that made Dominick's eye twitch. Sensing his unnecessary panic, Tiffany grabbed his hand.

"It's all up to code. I promise," she said, smiling up at him. Dominick just nodded and squeezed her hand back. He noticed then that Brendan was gripping her other hand. Dominick didn't love it, but there was nothing he could do. When the smoke cleared, seven drag queens were standing around the stage. Dominick was familiar enough with the drag world, thanks to social media. He could tell their makeup was very well done and the wigs they had on, white and towering with candies and gifts sticking out of them, would have cost a grip on Earth.

A Black drag queen in a floor-length glittery gown stepped to the stage and, just as the lyrics to "Sleigh Ride" kicked in, they all began lip-syncing over The Ronettes' classic vocals. The place went wild. Soon though, the lyrics dropped out and the drag queen in question addressed the crowd.

"Citizens of Whoville!" she joked. "I am The First Noelle and these are my girls, the rest of the Noelles." The queens behind her executed a little two-step in unison. Dominick and the rest of the crowd ate it up. "The beauty of the North Pole is its beautiful elves, its wonderful children and the creatures who honor us with their wisdom and company. We come from all over the world, every walk of life, but only a select few of us arrive here with the gift of the gag. Okay, honey?!

"We have a new elf—a new *queen* in our midst. One who gave her life saving one of our elders on the streets of New York. Her selflessness and her bravery put her in the running to be our new Santa Claus, but one look at Miss Shauna Chantal over there... Uh huh, we see you girl."

Dominick searched the crowd and saw Shauna on the other side of the stage, covering her cheeks.

"She took one look at you and said 'Oh no, I know why I am here and who I am working to please.' Though the title of loooove slave does sound appealing, our newest edition will join our caretaker elves in looking after our precious children and finally, *finally* bringing drag story hour to the North Pole. With no further delay, some of you may know him by his government name Christopher Ahn, but we will know him as the lovely, the charming, the hilarious, the stunning, Metro! Bang! And his new duck companion, Quackie O."

Dominick blinked as more fireworks erupted around the stage. The Noelles parted and another drag queen appeared. Even though Dominick knew exactly what was going on, he was not ready to see all six feet of Chris in full pageant-queen drag. Chris was a good looking dude, but MetroBang! was something to behold. MetroBang! worked the stage, taking over the lead lip syncing on "Sleigh Ride" with that ridiculous duck bouncing around under her arm.

It was a damn good performance. After the final notes

rang out, MetroBang! took her bow, not out of breath, and with tears sparkling in her eyes. Dominick had never been happier for someone else. Chris was absolutely in his element and the joy radiating from him was palpable.

"Thank you all for such a beautifully warm welcome. Mrs. Claus," he held his hand toward Tiffany, "thank you for extending this gracious offer to me. And to all the kids, thank you for letting me be a part of this world with you. I know we have so much to learn from each other and I can't wait to share more stories with you and hear everything you have to share with me."

"We love you!" Tiffany shouted back. Chris's smile widened and then he looked at Dominick before his gaze swept over to Brendan and Jeffery. Dominick glanced over, seeing the way Jeffery was fighting back tears. He gave Chris a thumbs up before he went back to clapping along with the music. Whatever was going on with Brendan was less clear. His jaw was tense and Dominick wasn't sure it was from the raw excitement of the moment or if Brendan was pissed. He'd been raised in a religious cult. Maybe seeing Chris as MetroBang! was too much for him.

"I have no idea what life was like before my fellow would-be Santas and I arrived, but you all have three very special guys here. Whoever takes the sleigh, as it were, will make you very proud." Chris fell right back into the choreography as he picked up the last portion of the lyrics. He finished with a flourish, tossing Quackie O into the sky. Thankfully the duck remembered she had wings and flapped her way into Brendan's arms.

The celebration only lasted one more song, Stevie Wonder's rendition of "What Christmas Means to Me," with

MetroBang! and the Noelles really putting in an ensemble effort to entertain the crowd. After, The First Noelle dismissed the crowd, encouraging everyone to take their time over the coming days to introduce themselves to Chris and Quackie O.

Chris floated off the stage and made his way over to them. He had magic now. Dominick knew he was an elf, but it still shocked him for a moment. Tiffany was the first to rush over to him.

"That was spectacular," she gushed.

"Thank you. I was so nervous, but the Noelles took great care of me."

"That was quite the show," Jeffery added, smiling wide. "The North Pole is lucky to have you."

"You're not still mad at me and my foul mouth?" Chris joked.

"Nah. It was a clever ruse. Now I know you were just winding me up."

"You enjoy the show?" Chris asked Brendan.

"I did. What's it called? Your face is beat to the gods?"

"Yes! You get it!"

"A lot of my students loved the *Drag Race*. But, uh, when did this all happen?" Brendan asked, still holding Quackie. He was definitely on edge. His face could have been bright red from all the excitement, but Dominick didn't think that was it.

"Sorry I couldn't let you in on the secret, big guy. It was kind of spur of the moment and I wouldn't be me if I didn't make an entrance."

"That's true. Well, congrats. It feels like you belong here."

"Congratulations, man," Dominick said, pulling him into a tight hug. "The kids need someone like you."

"Thanks, man," Chris replied, before glancing over his shoulder and leading Dominick a few feet away. "I just want you to know that I threw my vote in your hat."

"Is there an actual vote?" Dominick asked, a little shocked.

"No. From what I could get out of Harvey, it sounds like the Spirit of Christmas makes the final call based on who will be best for all of the North Pole and all of the Santa believers, so just, like, two billion people. No big deal. But still, I told Tiffany, Harvey and the Spirit this morning when she welcomed me that it has to be you."

"What makes you say that?"

Chris bit the corner of his lip, like he was trying to decide between a good comeback or the truth. "It's pretty simple actually. You love her."

"Hmm."

"And you're not denying it. Come on, I have to find Shauna. If she didn't like the show, I need to rethink all of my afterlife choices."

"Hey. If it's not me," Dominic said, "you look after her, okay?"

"You really are a prince. Come on."

33

Tiffany was so happy with how everything had worked out. Chris was happy. Dominick and the guys were happy for him. Shauna was definitely happy. The mood all around Santa's village felt right and she had Chris to thank for that. Still, there was a job to be done and three more prospective Santas who needed her attention. She leaned forward in their little conversation circle and put her hand on Chris's arm.

"Sorry to interrupt, but I have to keep this Santa party going."

"Of course. Thank you again."

"Thank you. We don't have to hold a job fair this month," she replied with a wink. "Harvey?"

"Yes, ma'am?"

"Can you show Jeffery and Brendan to the wood shop? I'm going to spend the afternoon with Dominick."

"It would be my pleasure," Harvey replied.

"Brendan, I will be by the cottage later to pick you up for a little dinner date."

"Can't wait," he replied. Tiffany hadn't forgotten what Dominick had told her Farrah had said about Brendan being out of place here. She could be right or he could be Santa. Spending some time alone with him would make things clearer and if things went his way, that clarity would make it somewhat easier to let Dominick go. Okay, that wasn't true at all, but lying to herself was the best she could do at the moment.

"Wonderful. Chris, you're in great hands with the Noelles and Lee-Ann. I'm so glad to say I'll see you around."

"Me too."

Tiffany turned to Dominick and held out her hand. "Shall we?" She tried not to make it so obvious that holding his hand made her feel a million times better, but she couldn't ignore the way Brendan was practically tracking their fingers as they laced together.

"We'll see you guys later," Dominick said as he led her out of the fray. "I have no idea where we're going, so maybe you should be walking in front of me," he added, stopping in front of the Post Office.

"Around the square, toward the crafting barn and then take a sharp left."

"On it." Dominick tucked her behind his body and used his size and imposing presence to part the crowd like a polite cowcatcher. He greeted everyone they passed with a warm "Hello, how you doing?" He was smart not to stop once, lest they be trapped in the village square all day, just chatting away. Tiffany heard a few surprised giggles and "Oh hello, Mrs. Claus!" more than a few times, once people realized she was speed walking behind Dominick's hulking frame. Very quickly, they were taking that left down Sleigh Bells Lane.

The street was much calmer and quieter, with only a handful of elves who were heading back to work.

"Where to now?"

"Straight ahead and to the right when the lane splits. You'll see when we get down there."

Dominick skidded to a halt and turned to face her. "Should I pick you up and run? I feel like this is gonna be good."

"No!" Tiffany laughed. "Just keep walking."

"Ah, okay." A few minutes later, they turned onto Sprite's Circle and were standing right in front of their destination. Santa's Garage. Tiffany watched Dominick's face as the recognition dawned on him.

"I wasn't exactly hiding this place from the other guys, but I feel like it would be more important to you."

"Ya damn right! Can we go inside?"

"No. We are gonna stand out here. You're gonna close your eyes, I'm going to describe all the vehicles inside in great detail and then we are going to a four-hour sewing tutorial."

"Look, I wanna know how to sew beyond sutures, so don't tempt me with a good time, but I gotta get inside that garage."

"Come on, you goof." Tiffany tugged him forward, using her magic to slowly roll open the elephant doors. She'd requested that all the transpo elves steer clear of the garage until further notice. Of course they'd followed her orders, but she hadn't expected them to go all out on the presentation.

All the popular sleighs from the last one hundred and fifty years were stationed in a semi-circle around the garage, with the special prototype she'd asked them to put together just for Dominick at the center.

Tiffany didn't say anything at first, just watching as he looked around, seemingly unsure where to start first.

"I wouldn't say there's a new sleigh every year, but it's close. These are the best ones we have."

She'd expected Dominick to make a beeline for the center of the room, where his prototype was bathed in sunshine coming from the open skylight. Instead, he walked over to the original sleigh, crafted from Italian green oak. She followed closely behind as he carefully looked over each sleigh. He didn't ask any questions or say anything, really. He just seemed to be basking in the beauty and the craft of each vehicle.

Finally, he stopped at the last sleigh in Laurence's collection.

"This is slick," he said, walking around the rear.

"The elves asked Laurence if he wanted to go after a more modern look, but he was stuck on this one."

"I can see why." Dominick lightly trailed his fingers over the curve of the trunk.

"He said there was this gangster who had a 'honey' and a couple kids in his neighborhood. He used to come around and bring all the kids on their street toys and sweets when he came to check on them. He remembered everything about his car. It was a white 1936 Packard Roadster." Tiffany used her magic to bring up a photo of the actual car and handed it to him. "We figured candy apple red would suit Santa's needs a little bit better."

"I would be a menace in this car," Dominick said, handing the photo back.

"I can see that," Tiffany laughed and then a strange feeling came over her. The tug in her chest was back and much stronger. "Can I tell you something silly?"

"Of course. I'm always down to clown. Lay it on me."

"I feel like you're my boyfriend," Tiffany confessed, her cheeks warming and her nose scrunching up from embarrassment. Her body heated a little lower as Dominick ran his tongue over his canine, looking her up and down, nice and slow.

"Who says I'm *not* your boyfriend?" he said. If she lost him, Tiffany would ask Gabriel to bottle the rough strokes of his deep voice just for emergencies.

"But that would mean I'm your girlfriend."

"You are. You're my lady and I'm your man. It's just that your *job* is making you link up with a side piece, but it seems like you and I both know what the deal is."

"I think so."

"Good."

Tiffany's mind and heart started searching for conflicted feelings and dread, but she couldn't find a hint of either. She liked being with Dominick, plain and simple, and maybe her head and her heart were finally in agreement. While she had him, knowing he wanted her too, it made no sense to waste a single moment harping on an end that may or may not come. She had to be present with him now. Tiffany leaned against the sleigh, crossing her arms under her breasts. She didn't miss the way Dominick's gaze flicked from her cleavage back to her face.

"You know, I've never had a boyfriend before," she said. This flirting thing was fun.

"Oh, is that right?"

"Yup and, I'm curious. As my boyfriend, if it weren't for

this pesky *job*, how would you handle things next?" It was a silly question, but as long as she was keeping the dread at bay, she might as well give herself a hint of the fantasy.

"Hmmm. After a while—I don't know, a week or two—I'd ask you to be my wife. On our terms, of course."

"Just a week or two?"

"Tiffany, I'm trying to give us time for this thing to grow. Please."

"Okay," she laughed. "Go on."

"I'd have to figure out where the jeweler is around here and get you a ring. I'd hope you'd say yes."

"And after that?"

"Despite what you said about the magic of this place, if you were on board, we'd work really, really hard to make a North Pole baby or two. Or three."

"How hard are we talking?"

"Mrs. Claus, I am talking hours and hours of hard, sweaty work. It might take us months or years to get that kind of magic on our side."

"I think it would be worth it. Did you ever think about being a dad?" she asked.

Dominick shook his head, a sad smile spreading over his face. "I never really thought about having a family of my own, but Farrah and Waltie are making me think I would have enjoyed being a dad. What I could have had if I had taken myself more seriously as a man. I'd definitely enjoy spending more time with them and the rest of the kids. But I know I'd be happy with any kind of future with you. Our own kids, afterlife angel kids, talking dogs and a line-stepping skunk—"

"You know she ratted us out to Shauna?"

"What?" he laughed.

"Yup. Told her I snuck you through the closet."

"Oh, well if Shauna knows what's good, then we really don't have to sneak around, do we?" Dominick wrapped his arm around her waist and pulled her close. Tiffany went willingly, pressing her lips to his.

"Come on. You need to see this one up close." She took his hand and led him over to the prototype. Another classic, with sleek lines and curves, but nothing like the design they'd taken off the Packard. "If you stay, we could make something like this."

"It looks familiar, but I can't place it," he said, looking inside at the dashboard's navigation tracker and chrome mounts for the reins. The sleigh had chrome accents all around, its vibrant red body mounted on chrome rails.

"There was a man who lived down the street from your first apartment," she started.

Dominick turned to her. "Mr. Price."

"Mr. Price."

"He had a 69 Cadillac Eldorado. His was black and this..."

"I mean, we'd tweak it or come up with something completely different. If you like it, why don't you try it out? Climb inside."

Dominick let go of her hand and climbed into the driver's seat. Its shiny piped leather had a holly leaf accents stitched into it. The back compartment was plenty big for Santa's sack of toys. She watched as he tested the give in the bench before he stretched out his long legs. Plenty of room for him.

"Dasher and Dancer know the way, and they'll teach you everything you need to know to drive it and fly with ease," Tiffany explained.

"But this only seats one, huh?"

"Well, on the night, it's just you. No passengers in the sleigh."

"I don't know if that would work. Come up here, Mrs. Claus"

Tiffany stepped up into the sleigh, letting Dominick guide her hips until she was leaning against the dashboard, standing between his legs. "Do you like it?" she asked, her tone turned breathy with desire. His strong, skilled fingers eased up her thighs, under the hem of her skirt. Her ruffled bloomers stopped him from reaching his prize, but Tiffany didn't mind one bit. She gasped as he pressed the quickly soaking fabric against her swelling center.

His eyes were trained on the work his fingers were doing, but for a split second he glanced up at her between his thick lashes. "You know I do. You don't need to change a thing." They both knew he wasn't talking about the sleigh.

34

Dominick knew they should be doing something more technical. He had more things to learn about the North Pole, more elves to meet, more questions he should ask about training with the reindeer and their flight paths, but he was perfectly happy spending all of their time together right there in the sleigh garage, his hands and his mouth all over Tiffany's body. On her insistence, she'd slid to the floor of the sleigh and taken him between her lips, licking and sucking until he couldn't handle it anymore. He'd pulled her onto his lap, so glad for that magic of hers that made her undershorts disappear. He'd taken her, rough and deep, losing his mind at the sounds she'd made, the echoes of her whimpers and cries bouncing off the high ceilings.

They were still in the sleigh, wet and tender parts exposed and ever ready for more, when the sun went down. He knew they were running out of time.

"Do you think I'd like Los Angeles? You know, in a human sense?"

"You might. I mean, it's hot as hell there, so you might

miss the snow, but you said you grew up on the water and we have a beach. People can't drive worth a damn, but I like it. Great Mexican food, great Asian cuisine from all over, great soul food if you know where to go. You'd like the vibe of Leimert Park and Inglewood. I'd have to take you to a show at the Forum. Not Sofi. That place is ass."

"I go down to the human world maybe once a decade, but I don't really hang around."

"You've got pretty sweet digs up here and all the cookies you can handle."

"That's true." He'd never get over the sound of her cute-ass laugh. "And you're up here now."

"I'm here now."

Tiffany sat up, lifting her head off his chest, and let out a frustrated sigh. Dominick ran his fingers down the back of her neck. She glanced over at him, looking so beautiful it threatened to cave his chest in.

"I have to go. Brendan is waiting."

"I know as a possible Santa, I need to let this rock, but as your boyfriend, I think Brendan needs to keep his hands to himself," he told her honestly. That gorgeous smile of hers lit up her face before she leaned over to kiss him.

"I'll make sure Mr. Kiffen keeps it PG." With a little fake cry, she stood, adjusted her dress and picked up her Santa hat from the floor of the sleigh, where it had fallen during round two of their x-rated exploration. Dominick zipped up his pants and, like she knew exactly how long to wait, Pepper appeared at the elephant doors.

"Looks like your trail guide is here," Tiffany teased.

"Always right on time. After your dinner with Brendan, my closet will be open, if you want to see me."

"I'll send Mrs. Skunk to get you."

"No." Dominick replied, dead serious.

Tiffany stood on her tiptoes, kissing him once more on the lips before she disappeared. Dominick looked around the garage, marveling at the masterful designs he may never see again before he took out the gold cell phone and sent an urgent text. Seconds later, he received an equally urgent reply. Dropping the phone back in his pocket, he gave Pepper a 'let's go' nod and the two of them headed back into the streets of Santa's village.

❄

Not five minutes later, they were in Harvey's office. It was a cozy space, fit for an elf who was barely five feet tall. Dominick felt like a giant standing on the other side of his size-proportionate desk, but it was fine. This conversation would be quick.

"What can I do?" he asked. "I care about this woman and I get it. There's the job. There's you guys. There's the kids. I get all of that and I want all of that, but I want to be with Tiffany. I know she can't be separated from the job, but I don't know. If it's not me, I don't want to leave her."

He wasn't quite begging, but he was ready to go there. He had fallen hard for Tiffany and, while he realized the afterlife was full of mysteries, he just couldn't rationalize going to a place called Heaven and never seeing her, never touching her again. Especially when he knew she wanted him back. "I feel like she's mine already and I'm definitely hers."

Harvey smiled, looking like he was about to shed a few tears. "Then just keep doing what you're doing."

"That's it? I can't enter a log chucking contest or challenge one of the local animals to a foot race?"

"Well, in this form, most of our creature residents can outrun you and we have two Highland Games champions on staff so no. But, I can tell you that Mrs. Claus's happiness is very important to all of us. If you truly care about her, then use your remaining time to make sure she knows that. I will happily report back to the team and share with them what you've told me just now."

"Thanks, I'd appreciate that."

"I took Brendan and Jeffery on quite the adventure this afternoon, so Jeffery requested dinner back at the cottage. You are free to join him or I'm sure Raymond and some of the other elves would be happy if you accompanied them to dinner."

"I'll come back out later, but I should probably go see what Jeffery's up to."

"Excellent. I'll see you and Miss Pepper soon."

Pepper nodded at Harvey in an eerily human way.

"I'd also like to stick around long enough to know what she's saying."

"She said thank you for meeting with us and she'd continue to look out for you," Harvey laughed.

"Oh. Okay then. Let's go, Pep." They left Harvey and his cozy office, and headed back into the snowy night.

35

Jeffery was right back at the dining room table, surrounded by a fresh stack of books, and this time he had two open in front of him. One was a thick volume with gilded edges and, at a quick glance, Dominick could see the other was a bible. Brendan was standing at the island in a full navy blue suit, eating from a very elaborate cheese platter.

"Fellas, how you doing?" Dominick asked as he took off his jacket. Pepper trotted past him and made herself comfortable in front of the roaring fire where a baby deer and a fox were fast asleep.

"Good. We had an interesting day," Jeffery replied. "How was your afternoon with Tiffany?"

"Can't complain. We checked out the sleighs. What was interesting about your day?"

"Encyclopedia Brown here means informative. I have had inquisitive students, but I've never heard someone ask so many questions," Brendan said, nodding in Jeffery's direction.

"We're here to learn a job that could be a centuries-long

appointment or longer. I think it's pretty important to know what's going on here."

"Yeah, that's fair, I guess."

"I think Brendan misses his friend Chris. He's been grumpy about it all day."

"That was a pretty impressive reveal," Dominick replied as he headed toward the sink and started washing his hands. He wanted to get in on that cheese platter. As soon as the water touched his fingers, Dominick felt Brendan lean a little too far into his personal space. Dominick jerked away as he felt Brendan's hot breath on his ear.

"That's probably a good idea, washing your hands. I can smell her all over you."

Dominick glared back at Brendan, a flash of anger heating the front and back of his neck. He spent a split second debating whether or not to punch Brendan in the face before a weird-ass look passed over Brendan's brow. Dominick's eyes narrowed even more.

"I don't think you should be worried about me," Dominick said real slow. After a long moment, Brendan just replied with one of those 'maybe, maybe not' shrugs and turned back to the assortment of crackers on the island. Dominick swallowed and went back to the task at hand, his body still tensed. He officially didn't trust Brendan. When he turned and walked to the other side of the island, keeping the slab of wood and granite between them, it seemed like Jeffery had missed the whole interaction. He looked up from his book, ready for another round of philosophizing.

"I think Chris's decision should be very helpful to all of us."

"I think it's a cop out," Brendan replied.

"How so?" Dominick asked, still considering that punch.

"He knew he wasn't going to get the Santa gig, so he found a loophole so he could stay."

"I disagree," Jeffery said. "I think Chris had as good a chance as the rest of us, but he showed us that we have more choice than we initially thought in the situation. He wants to work in the North Pole and we also learned that it is perfectly acceptable for us to develop feelings in the afterlife. I wish him and Shauna the best."

"Whatever," Brendan grumbled.

Dominick stood there, really thinking about what Jeffery had just said. It was clear that Jeffery was not thinking about Tiffany in any romantic way and he was solely focused on the professional requirements of the job, not the emotional ones. At the same time, he was right about Chris. Chris had made a choice and Tiffany, for him, had never been an option. Dominick couldn't relate, but it was something to think about when it came to Jeffery and Brendan. If they weren't holding real feelings for Tiffany, that could change things.

Dominick glanced toward the pantry, deciding to let Brendan handle the cheese and crackers.

"Jeffery, if I made a cast iron pizza, would you be into that?"

"That sounds great. After, I want to walk back down to the village. Dasher said she would meet me there and show me the runway. Did you see it?"

"Ah, no."

"He was busy," Brendan said.

"That's fine," Jeffery replied. "It's probably better to see it at night. She said take off is always after dark."

"Hey, man. Are you cool?" Dominick asked Brendan.

"Yeah. I'm good," his tone cool, like he wasn't being an absolute asshole.

"Good." Dominick headed into the pantry, glad Brendan would be leaving for his date any minute, and pissed that that date was with Tiffany. If he was still coming with this attitude when he got back, Dominick would set him straight. Just as he stepped back into the kitchen, his arms loaded down with most of the things he needed for dinner, there was a knock at the door. A second later, Tiffany's beautiful face peeked in.

"Hello? May I come in?"

"Of course," Dominick said. He had to stop himself from making his way over to her and kissing her on the mouth. She stepped inside, showing off her outfit change. She was wearing a waist-hugging coat dress that fell below her knees in green velvet, with a deep, v-neck, fur-trimmed collar and fur lining the cuffs. She looked amazing.

"Good evening, Tiffany. How are you doing?"

"I'm well, Jeffery. Thank you for asking. I'm here to pick up my date." She gave Brendan a warm smile that his bitch ass did not deserve. "And tomorrow morning, I figured the four of us could have brunch. After, the kids want to put on a mini Christmas play for you."

"Can't wait," Dominick replied. Jeffery nodded in agreement.

"Wonderful." Tiffany held out her hand for Brendan. "Sir, our car is waiting."

"Later, chumps. Don't wait up."

Tiffany's laugh was the only thing that kept Dominick from punching him in the back of his head. He watched as Brendan walked over to her and slipped an arm around her waist. He went in for a kiss, but Tiffany deftly dodged his lips, offering her cheek instead. Dominick couldn't see his face when he pulled away from the friendly peck, but Tiffany seemed to soothe him with a hand on his big chest.

"Goodnight, you two." Tiffany said before they headed out the door.

Dominick let out a deep breath as the door closed. He wasn't sure he'd be able to distract himself until he saw Tiffany again, but he'd do his best.

"Jeffery, you want—" A weird noise coming from outside stopped his voice in his throat. Jeffery's head popped up and all the animals by the fire were suddenly awake.

"I mean it, Brendan! Stop!"

Dominick sprinted for the door, Jeffery right on his heels. He ripped the door open, his vision going red when he saw Tiffany struggling in Brendan's arms against the back of a bright red Escalade. Before they could get across the porch, Tiffany used her magic to vanish out of his grip, reappearing a good ten yards away.

"What is wrong with you?!" she shouted at him and Brendan didn't say anything. He let out an inhuman snarl, his body tensing like he was about to make the unwise decision to go after her again. Tiffany could clearly hold her own, but something was fucking off, beyond his unwanted groping.

Slowly, Brendan turned his gaze toward the porch and Dominick saw it. Brendan's eyes were glowing red and his teeth turned to bright yellow fangs. Tiffany could use her magic to take Brendan, but she might not be able to handle whatever the hell had possessed him. Those glowing eyes flashed in Dominick and Jeffery's direction, a challenge from whatever was inside Brendan. It wasn't done with Tiffany yet.

36

Later, Dominick could ask Jeffery how they'd moved so in sync, but in that moment, all that mattered was that they did. As they both leapt off the porch, something strong and warm propelled Dominick forward like a guiding hand on his back. He felt that push penetrate deeper just as Brendan pounced. Brendan didn't make it very far, though, because Jeffery slammed his whole body into him, knocking Brendan into a snow drift on the far side of the driveway. In that same moment, Dominick made it to Tiffany, wrapping her in a sudden magic of his own, which didn't make sense. Still, they reappeared together on the porch.

He looked her over, checking her face and body for any obvious sign of injury. His heart was pounding triple time in his chest, wrapped in a deep sense of joy and celebration that he had to force himself to ignore until he knew his baby was out of danger. *Let her be okay. Please, let her be unharmed.* "Are you okay? Did he hurt you?"

"No, sweetie. I'm fine. I—" her breath caught as she looked up at his face. "Dominick, you're—"

"Tiffany! I'm sorry!" Brendan called out.

Their attention was immediately drawn across the yard to where Gabriel had appeared, golden wings unfurled, with a flaming sword at Brendan's throat. His fire-lit eyes were still glowing red and his yellow fangs were visible. Tiffany started down the porch stairs and Dominick grabbed her hand.

"Wait."

She turned back to him, a cautious smile soothing his heart. "It's okay. Come on. Look." Dominick followed her, crossing the yard. The angel holding Brendan at bay wasn't Gabriel. It was Jeffery.

"Get him off me!" Brendan cried out. "I didn't mean to—I just—" They eased closer as Brendan started to whimper, the heat from the sword singeing his throat. Jeffery didn't let up.

"He gave himself to Krampus," he said through gritted teeth.

"Brendan," Tiffany replied. "Why?"

"I knew it wasn't me. It's always been him," he hissed, nodding in Dominick's direction. The sword burned some hairs off his beard as he moved. Just then, the ground started to rumble and a telltale cloud of dark smoke appeared, bringing the asshole in question. Karl looked around, just as shocked and confused at the rest of them. His gaze went from Brendan and Jeffery to Tiffany and Dominick, then back to Brendan again.

"What the fuck happened, Brendan?"

"I don't know. I fucked up."

"He knows." Tiffany said, any ounce of grace she had

clearly drying up. "He tried to force himself on me after I said no, just because I wouldn't let him kiss me."

Dominick moved to strangle Brendan himself, but Karl beat him to it. Krampus's tail flicked out and whipped Brendan across the cheek with its spiked tip. Brendan screamed, the fresh stripe on his face bleeding and boiling. The sound of his cries were drowned out when that same tail wrapped around his throat and squeezed.

"Dumbass. My apologies, Mrs. Claus. Santa." He bowed in front of Tiffany, then turned toward Dominick and repeated the gesture. "I didn't know a choice had already been made. I simply offered Brendan a position with me, just like the rest. I had a feeling he was going to accept, but he knew the rules."

"And he didn't follow them," Dominick heard over his shoulder. He turned and was faced with a sudden blinding light as Gabriel, Jubilee and Oliver flew over the cottage roof, the heavenly trio touching down on gilded wings. Jeffery stood at attention, his sword extinguished as he tucked it behind his back. Gabriel took in the scene, a hint of a smile touching his face as he looked in Dominick's direction. It disappeared immediately when he laid eyes on Tiffany. Gabriel came over and took her hand.

"Did he hurt you?"

"He tried, but I'm unharmed. He just scared me. I thought he was a good guy. Apparently not!" she yelled the last part in Brendan's direction.

"Tiffany. Please, I'm sorry."

"Yeah, apology not accepted," she grumbled, moving closer to Dominick's side. He didn't waste a moment, putting his arm around her and tucking her against his chest. If he had his way, Brendan and Karl would never breathe the same air as her again.

Oliver took Brendan's hand and made the pathetic jackass stand as Gabriel went right over to Karl. "I think you claimed your acolyte ahead of schedule."

Karl at least had the sense to cower in front of Gabriel. "I have no excuse. He leapt prematurely. His jealousy and desire were clear, but I thought he had them under control and I was wrong. I was going to teach him how to focus it."

"He'll have to be punished. You both will."

"No!" Brendan wheezed. "Please—"

"Silence."

"He is yours, Karl, but he's banished from the North Pole. Forever." Brendan had the sense to finally keep his mouth shut, but he sobbed at Gabriel's order, sooty tears running down his face. Gabriel ignored him and went on. "Mr. and Mrs. Claus will decide how long it will be before you yourself enter the North Pole again. Your visitation status is revoked."

"Of course," Karl said. "Those terms are acceptable to me, if they are acceptable to the two of you."

In the back of his mind and in his heart, Dominick knew that Gabriel and Karl were talking to him and Tiffany as a unit. He knew the force that lived inside him now, that had carried him across the driveway and given him the magic to pull Tiffany to safety, was the Spirit of Christmas. Essee had bonded with his heart and his soul, which meant he was Santa. But, it felt like a distant truth and hadn't sunk in yet.

He turned to Tiffany, who reached up and stroked his beard. His hand rose in kind, brushing across her soft cheek. "It's your call, Mrs. Claus. Whatever you want."

Tiffany smiled for a moment, before she turned a mean-ass glare back on Karl. "I never want to see you again. You and Dominick can work out your own schedule. You and I, and all your minions, no longer have any business."

"I accept," Karl said with a nod.

"I know you do. You don't have a choice. Goodbye Karl."

He nodded again before he stepped back over to Brendan, driving his claws into the back of his neck. They disappeared together, this time in a small cloud of smoke without all the fanfare and earth shaking.

"Gabriel, not to question your methods, but I'm not sure sending Brendan where he ultimately wanted to go is much of a punishment," Dominick said.

Oliver chimed in. "He chose Krampus as a last resort. He wasn't ready to move on, but he thought it was his only chance to stay close to Mrs. Claus. I felt it in his heart. The last place he wants to be is with Karl."

"Plus, you gotta remember, Karl's a demon," Gabriel added. "His realm smells so bad. Brendan will be regretting all of his choices the second he breathes in through his nose."

Dominick couldn't argue with that. Karl's breath was rancid. If his Krampus Kingdom smelled anything like that, Brendan was in for a lifetime of pain.

"We have to be going. We weren't due here for another few days and now we have a new angel to welcome," Gabriel said, before he turned to Jeffery. "We'll give you a few minutes."

"Thank you."

Gabriel and Oliver took off immediately, flying into a sudden, bright light above. Jubilee hung back for a moment before she walked over to Dominick and gave his chin a waggle, like she was an adoring grandma. Then, she turned to Tiffany.

"I picked this one just for you," Jubilee said.

"Thank you. He's pretty cute," Tiffany replied.

"Isn't he? You two take care of each other."

"We will, I promise," Dominick told her. Jubilee winked at them and made a dramatic show of jumping on top of the Escalade before her wings carried her off into the night. Finally, it was just the two of them and Jeffery, the chill of the night and fresh snowflakes surrounding them. He walked over.

"Tiffany—"

"You don't need to explain."

"I—being here, I realized the universe is just so big and there's so much to do. So many people to look after. I want to be put to good use."

"And you will be. You were fit for those golden wings."

"Yeah, they look good on you, man," Dominick added.

Jeffery turned in Dominick's direction and pulled him into a tight embrace. Dominick laughed, trying to wrap his arms around his massive wings. "You were the better man, right from the beginning," Jeffery said. "The Spirit of Christmas made the right choice." As if she agreed, Essee hummed within Dominick's chest.

"I hope I live up to the job."

"You will. Look, Harvey and Shauna are on their way, and so are the animals. I should go. You two talk to them. But, I'll be back," Jeffery said.

"Okay," Tiffany replied, a little choked up. He stepped clear of the car and the porch, letting his wings unfold.

Dominick and Tiffany watched as he took flight, disappearing into his own bright light in the sky.

37

Now that the proverbial dust and the literal sulfur had settled, Dominick knew exactly what he needed to do. Essee was showing him the way, guiding him from within. He had to meet with the elves, formally reintroduce himself to all the children and commune with the animals. There would be a celebration, a mid-year festival just for him, and at some point along the way, with no formality whatsoever, he and Tiffany would be husband and wife. He looked down at her as she looked at the burnt trail in the snow where Jeffery's sword had nearly ended things for Brendan. She glanced up at the sky, where the angels had been moments before, then she looked at him.

Dominick didn't need to ask her what was wrong because he knew. Her adrenaline was still pumping. She was overwhelmed and in shock. Brendan had violated her trust and her kindness, Karl had crossed too many lines and suddenly, she had a new Santa. It was a lot to take in. Dominick wasn't processing it well either.

Gently, he took Tiffany's hand and led her to the porch steps, where Pepper and the baby deer were waiting. Dominick took a seat on the top step and pulled Tiffany between his legs. She sank down on the step below him and draped her arms over his thigh, resting her head. Dominick ran his fingers down her velvet-covered back, trying his best to soothe her.

He could feel more animals approaching, but he turned and looked at Pepper.

"Where were you during all that? You couldn't gnaw an ankle or something?" he asked, knowing he would finally understand her. She didn't move her mouth when she responded, instead telegraphing her voice into his head.

"I figured the angel with the flaming sword had things under control," she replied. Tiffany snorted at her response while Dominick was confused by the fact that Pepper had an Eastern European accent.

"Yeah. You right." He had more questions for Pepper, but they'd have to wait for another time.

Dominick saw movement in the trees and a moment later, Shadow trotted out from between the firs. She didn't say anything, just came right up the steps and rested her head on Tiffany's foot. More creatures followed. Dasher and all the reindeer, two polar bears and six cubs, Mrs. Fox and Mrs. Rabbit. Three barn owls and a handful of chickadees landed on top of the SUV. Mrs Skunk, that rat, pattered out of the trees with eight adorable skunk babies toddling behind her.

Dominick should have been shocked by the penguins or the entire wolf pack that made their way out of the trees, but they fit right in. The wildlife parade didn't seem to end until two eagles, one golden and one bald, swooped down and landed on the porch posts.

"They've come to honor you," Tiffany said quietly.

"Thank you," was all Dominick could say. The creatures seemed fine with that. They were waiting for Harvey anyway. A few moments later, the man in question came walking up the driveway, carrying a staff made of twisted wood. Chris and Shauna were hurrying right behind him, carrying what looked to be a golden tray and a snow globe. The animals made room for the trio to reach the porch. Tiffany stood and pulled him up with her, so they could greet them.

"We three Kings—" Chris joked. Dominick let out a snort of his own, glad the elf life hadn't changed his friend. Shauna handed over the tray-like item, which was actually a large mirror.

"Thought you might want that."

"Thanks." Dominick wasn't sure what she was talking about until he held the mirror up and got a glimpse of his new look. He turned his head to look at the new points that topped his ears. His beard, his mustache and his fade were all pure white. He didn't look old, he looked otherworldly. He looked like Santa.

"In the past, they found the makeover reveal is best done with other people around. Our last Santa fainted."

"He did," Tiffany giggled.

"No worries, I look good," Dominick said, handing the mirror back. He turned and gave his attention to Harvey, who seemed anxious as hell, no longer the calm, jovial elf he'd spoken to less than an hour ago.

"Gabriel sent us a message and let us know the Spirit of

Christmas has made her choice," Harvey said, handing the staff over with a bow. "Our Santa selection is complete."

"Appreciate it." Dominick took the staff and tried not to roll his eyes. Tiffany had tried to tell him that Santa was basically king of the North Pole, the center of everything. Dominick was more than ready to handle the responsibilities, but everyone didn't need to start treating him differently just because he'd be given a supernatural dose of Just For Men, silky white.

"We have to present you in the village and then I'm sure the children will want to talk to you. After, I think we need to hear exactly what happened with Brendan and Jeffery. Gabriel didn't share any details. If you'll follow me back to your workshop, we can get you—"

Dominick stopped him. "Harvey. We're not doing this right now. Tomorrow, I'll do whatever you want. Full parade, commencement speech, PowerPoint presentation, trust falls, dance offs, Black Friday forty percent off sale, whatever. But Tiffany and I need tonight."

Harvey blinked and looked over at Tiffany like he was seeing her for the first time and that pissed Dominick off. Just hours ago, he was showing her respect and deference, and now he barely noticed her.

"Of course. Mrs. Claus. I'm sorry, I'm a little flustered."

"It's okay, Harvey. Tomorrow would definitely be better," Tiffany said.

"Of course."

"I'm going to take Mrs. Claus home," Dominick said before he nodded over his shoulder. "Pepper can give you the details of how this all went down."

"I'd be happy to," Pepper agreed.

"Okay, then. Tomorrow," Harvey replied.

Dominick nodded. "Tomorrow." He turned to Tiffany, smoothing her soft hair over her elfen ears. She looked at him, a small smile touching the corner of her lips. Dominick handed the staff back to Harvey and wrapped his arms around his girlfriend. Using his magic, he carried them out of there in a gust of wind and snow.

38

The moment they landed in their quarters, Dominick knew he'd made the right decision. He had a laundry list of shit to deal with, but Tiffany was still on edge and she came first. She stepped out of his arms and walked into the great room. She lit the fire with her mind, *Firestarter* style, and started pacing the room. Dominick used his magic to conjure a fire screen for the hearth. Tiffany chuckled a little and kept right on pacing. She knew who she picked.

"I'll go over to Krampusville and kill Brendan myself," Dominick offered and he meant it. He and Karl could have it out, and he was sure Gabriel wouldn't mind in any real way that mattered.

Tiffany waved him off. "I don't care about Brendan. He just scared me for a moment. I was stressing myself out, trying to give him a fair shake, and it turns out that wasn't necessary at all. That creep."

"Then come here. Let me hold you for a second. It's been a weird night."

"No," she said, with an almost comical frown. "I need to move around."

"Will you at least talk to me?"

She stopped right in front of the fire, anger and confusion blazing across her face. "Okay, I'll talk. I don't understand this."

"What do you mean?"

"I don't understand how Essee picked you and I don't understand how Karl got to Brendan so easily."

"Did you want it to be Brendan standing here?" Dominick asked.

"No, of course not. I wanted you and that's what I don't understand. You saw Harvey back there. He almost forgot I was alive. I know he was shocked too, but you—Santa—I tried to explain it. *You* are the fixture. You're the star and I'm here to help you. You even saw how quickly Karl changed his tune once the decision was made. What I want doesn't matter. I *never* get what I want, especially when it comes to *you*."

"Okay, first off, whatever was happening before? I don't want that. I don't want Mrs. Claus to be a glorified assistant. I want *you*. I want to be your husband and Harvey knows that."

"I don't know." Tears started trailing down her cheeks. "Maybe they wanted me to find a 'love match' so the process would go smoother."

Dominick crossed the room and stopped right in front of her. "Tiff, I don't care. I want you and, as long as you want me too, that's all that matters. I told Harvey it was you and me or nothing. He knows what the deal is, even if all he truly cares about is the job. But, can *you* believe *me*? Can you believe how I feel about you? About us?"

Tiffany peered up and scrutinized him until she finally nodded. "I just don't get it. Why would they give me what I want?"

"Who cares? We're together now and that's what matters. Also, that offer for Brendan is still on the table," Dominick replied, very seriously. Tiffany laughed, wiping her eyes. "Look, it's been a strange, yet perfectly erotic couple of days for me, but you've been here for hundreds of years. I won't pretend I know what you're feeling right now, but just know that I want to be here with you. I want to be here *because* of you. We'll be The Clauses. Not Santa and his trusty wife."

More tears left the corners of her eyes as she nodded again. "Okay."

"I'm sure it's going to take some time for us both to adjust. You're in denial about all the sex we're gonna have," he said, glad he was able to get a chuckle and a smile out of her. "I've never been married after two days before, but we'll figure it out. We just need some time." Dominick searched inside, looking for Essee to offer some sort of contradiction, but she was in agreement. They belonged together and time was on their side.

"I know. You're right. I just—" Tiffany sighed, then finally gave up and put her head on his chest. "It is hard to forget two hundred years of experience. You're right, though. I just need some time."

"Tell me what you need tonight. You want something to eat? You want to take a bath? I saw that tub you got in there that fits like nine people. You want me to sex you up? I'll sex you up real good. You could teach me how to sew. I bet I could learn real fast with all these magical powers I have now. Or how about I do things right and propose."

Dominick dropped down on one knee and used his magic to conjure a round diamond solitaire ring. He slipped it on Tiffany's finger, as she tried to hide her tears and her laugh with her other hand.

"I'm actually more of an Asscher-cut girl."

"I should have asked. My bad." Dominick immediately changed the stone and made it a little bigger. He stood and took Tiffany's cheeks between his hands, kissing her softly on the lips. "I'm not going anywhere. Now tell me what you need tonight."

"I want a soft pretzel and a coke float," she said with an adorable pout.

"Piece of cake. What else?"

"I wanna have sex with you in the tub and then I want to cuddle in bed."

"Geez, being married to you is going to be really hard," he teased before he kissed her one more time.

❄

They followed the rest of the night to her exact specifications. Kissing and touching him seemed to soothe Tiffany, so Dominick was more than willing when she told him she wanted to be on top. It was his pleasure to take her tits in his mouth while she created mini tidal waves in the water by grinding down on his shaft. The further they got away from the start of the night, the more Dominick started to settle more into his bond with the Spirit of Christmas. Essee was there if he needed wisdom or magic, but she felt more like his intuition, not at all the intrusion he'd been expecting. She understood that his main goal was loving Tiffany and she would do anything to support that, including drifting quietly into the background.

After the second time they made love, Tiffany told him more about what to expect in the coming days and he offered some Brendan-related revenge one more time. Tiffany was considering it. When she was satisfied with their soak, they headed back to their bedroom. Tiffany showed him his closet, which was now filled with clothes for him. He wasn't sure getting dressed was in the cards that night, but a knock on their door made the decision for them. Dominick slipped on a nice designer sweatsuit that would have cost him a few months pay back on Earth, then went to see if it was Harvey or Shauna.

He opened the door and found Waltie and close to two dozen elves. It took a second for him to realize they weren't just any elves. They were all firefighters, with emblems on their uniform t-shirts from New York, Boston, Cleveland, Portland, Phoenix, Chapel Hill, Miami-Dade and Baton Rouge. A young, light-skinned woman with hair slicked back in a regulation-style bun had LAFD stamped on her t-shirt. Dominick was lucky Waltie was there or he would have lost it. He let out a slow breath and then looked down at the little kid in front of him.

"Is there something I can help you with?" he teased Waltie.

"All the firefighters were looking for you. I know we'll have your party later, but they wanted to say hello, so I brought them here."

"Hmmm, I see. Well, thank you. I think this is the right group of people for me to meet right now."

"I'm gonna go back, so I don't miss story time with MetroBang!. Can I have a hug first?" Waltie asked.

Dominick laughed, an unfamiliar booming sound coming from deep in his chest, but he decided to roll with it as he scooped Waltie up. "Of course you can have a hug." He gave the kid a good squeeze and Waltie hugged his neck right back.

"I'm glad you stayed," he said.

"I am, too." He set Waltie down. After giving Dominick an adorable nod, he took off down the hall, weaving between the feet of the Nutcracker guards with Pepper, Shadow and two gray kittens on his heels. Once they'd disappeared around the corner, Dominick turned to the actual leader of this expedition. He was an older Black man, nearly Dominick's height with a thick handlebar mustache.

"Chief."

"Oh no, that's your title," the man replied, before he shook Dominick's hand. "Captain Russell Walker."

"Dominick Bell. Nice to meet all of you," he replied, just as Tiffany slipped under his arm, wrapped in a fluffy robe. Dominick pulled her close and felt the bursting emotions in him settle a bit when she rested her head on his chest.

"We all got Harvey's memo to leave you two alone for the night, but we've been hiding the last two days."

"I was gonna say, I walked all over the village and didn't see a firehouse anywhere."

"It's right next to the Cookie Emporium. We don't do much rescuing here. Mostly we handle any public event with fire or fireworks, plus any parades. What's a Christmas parade without the fire department? And of course, there's the chili."

"To keep things fair, we asked all the firefighters, football coaches and sanitation workers to stay out of sight. It took some convincing to get all the drag queens to go along with it, too. Ryan back there is also a Noelle," Tiffany explained.

"Hey Chief," a young white guy from Boston raised his hand.

"It's good to meet you all."

"We'll let you two get back to your evening, but we wanted you to have this," the young woman from Los Angeles said. She made her way forward and handed Dominick his helmet from the 94. It was like new, but Dominick suddenly remembered every moment, every call he'd worn it on his head. "Gabriel said he gave you the medal of valor you were owed, but you should have this too. You can keep them both in your office, whenever you get over there."

"Thank you," Dominick replied, emotion drying his throat.

"And this!" Ryan held up a sweatshirt with PROPERTY OF THE NORTH POLE FIRE BRIGADE printed on the front. He handed it over, making sure Dominick saw the words CHIEF BELL stitched onto the sleeve.

"We know you'll be busy with your primary gig, but you're always welcome at the firehouse," Captain Walker said.

"For sure. Thank you."

They said their goodbyes and Captain Walker led his crew back down the corridor.

"Do I have you to thank for this?" he asked Tiffany when they were back inside.

"No, that was all Russell. They are very happy it's you."

Dominick leaned down and kissed her on the lips. "I'm just surprised you were able to hide all those drag queens."

"It was a challenge, trust me."

39

Harvey may have been right about not needing to sleep as a citizen of the North Pole, but after settling into bed with Tiffany that night, Dominick fell into the most peaceful sleep he'd ever experienced. He felt whole with her by his side and comforted by the fact that Essee would guide him through his next steps as Santa. The sun was already up when he felt Tiffany moving in his arms. He was half awake, thinking about how to pitch the idea of a wedding, when he realized Tiffany and the bed were moving.

He sat straight up, trying to process what the hell he was seeing. Tiffany's whole body was emanating a warm glow, with black, white, silver and gold sparkling orbs seeming to light her from the inside out. Her eyes were still closed and there was this pleasant smile on her face, but something about it was all fucked up. Dominick reached for her, his hand unharmed as his fingers moved through the light. He gently shook her shoulder, praying she would wake up and just tell him she was in the middle of her morning skincare routine and he had nothing to worry about.

"Tiffany. Tiffany! Wake up!"

Her eyes snapped open, the whites replaced with glowing prisms, and her smile disappeared. She started screaming. "Dominick! No! No!"

He jumped off the bed and tried to pull her to him, but his hand went right through her. She was disappearing. "What the fuck is going on?"

"No!" she sobbed, reaching for his hand again with no chance of making contact. "They're calling me home. No. Dominick, I don't want to go."

"Tiffany—" Dominick had no idea what to do and, in the next second, Tiffany was gone.

40

Tiffany was being told not to panic, but she didn't know how that was possible. She'd finally found a man she loved and wanted to be with, and now she was being taken away from him. She closed her eyes against the blinding light obscuring the ground, which felt like it was rising up to meet her. Soon, the light eased and she could see. When she looked around, her fears were confirmed. The angels were calling her home.

She looked down the grassy bank of the Squamscott. All around her were new buildings and paved roads. The stables were gone and so were the old docks and the boat launch. But, when she peered across the river, the remains of the brick powder house were still there. Not a single person was in sight and she couldn't hear any cars. Looking over her shoulder, she saw a sign for Bette's Barbershop where Miller's Tavern used to be, and just behind it, she could see the stone foundation of her family's home. The house had an addition and a white coat of paint, but she'd recognize those large granite slabs anywhere.

Looking down at her hands, she realized the ring Dominick had given her was gone. Gabriel had brought her here to deliver the news. She had lost the job of Mrs. Claus. She had lost Dominick.

"Nothing is lost, my child," Tiffany heard a voice answer her unspoken fears in triplicate. She turned back to the water and saw Them coming toward her, glowing bronze skin, draped in bright purple and gold. Tiffany bowed her head and lowered her eyes. She'd only been in Their presence once before and she'd never forgotten the power of the experience.

"Do not hide your eyes from us. Come." Tiffany dared a glance and was met with a gaze filled with all the love and contradiction in the world. "Walk with us." She fell into step, bare feet in the grassy riverbank, and they began to walk.

"Did I do something wrong?" Tiffany asked.

"Of course not. We simply needed to call you to us. It has been many years. It is time you are given another choice."

They sent a wave of calm over her, but she was still so scared, so upset that it only kept her from hyperventilating. Tears streamed down her face.

"Dominick Bell," They said.

"Yes?"

"You care for him."

"Yes."

"But you do not trust your choice. You do not trust his choice. We want you to tell us why."

"I'm not sure what you mean. I want him, I love him, but I didn't choose him. The Spirit of Christmas chose him."

"Did she not choose him for you? Did she not choose him because he was the one you wanted? Did she not choose him because he stated his vow to you over and over again?"

"I don't understand."

"The lovers decided. You for him and he for you. Is that not enough?"

Tiffany stopped walking, which might have caused offense, but she felt like she was losing her mind. "A love match," she said. "But that never happened before. You never let me have that before."

"There was no mistake in choosing you as our winter princess," They said with a smile in Their voice. "But, we have learned over time that we should have eased you through the period of waiting. We should have let you know that, in time, your soul's mate would arrive. We waited for someone worthy of you. Laurence was sent to keep you company until your Dominick arrived. Dominick was given the same choices as the others, and at every turn, his only thoughts were of you."

"Oh," Tiffany said, still struck with disbelief. *How could it be so easy?*

"The years have been easy?" They asked with a twinkling laugh. Finally, Tiffany smiled.

"I have had so much fun. I love sharing the gift of Christmas. I love the children. I love the elves. I loved Laurence."

"But a piece was missing. Some are fine with community, care, adoration and purpose. Some want more."

"No. I'm sorry. It wasn't—it was enough. I loved them all and I felt loved."

"Now, my Tiffany. There is no reason to lie. Not to us. You all have different desires and different needs. The needs were part of your soul's creation and cannot be ignored. You need a companion to see you and treasure you. You need to feel that the special, overflowing love in your heart has found its perfect place. "

Tiffany had never thought of herself that way, but hearing it now, she knew it was true. She loved being Mrs. Claus. She loved the North Pole. And yet, she'd been incredibly lonely the whole time. "Yes," was all she could say.

"Your needs and desires matter to us. You yearn for a love and a family of your own, and we see that need. We apologize for not making that clear sooner."

Tiffany's mouth popped open. She quickly averted her eyes again and snapped her mouth shut. An apology was the last thing she'd expected, especially when she still felt she was to blame. She'd been given a whole world and still she wanted more. She was so confused.

"Over two hundred years is a long time, even for an immortal. So again, we will allow you to choose. Do you want to continue as Mrs. Claus?"

"Yes. Yes, I do!"

"And you want Dominick Bell to accompany you?"

"Yes! Please don't take him away from me. Please."

"Then speak your love out loud."

"I want to be with Dominick. I love him and I don't want to lose him. I want him to be the Santa to my Mrs. Claus."

"Then so it will be. Dominick Bell is a man of his word and you will have no reason to doubt that. We can see your mind still spinning, but do your best to listen when he speaks his love to you. Every word is true."

"Okay. Yes. Please let me keep him."

"He is yours, child," They laughed. "Return to him."

Tiffany froze as They approached her and pressed a delicate, yet powerful, hand on her belly and a glowing kiss to her forehead. Tiffany closed her eyes, feeling all their love and contradiction flowing through her body. When her gaze lifted, she was alone again on the banks of the Squamscott River and, in the next moment, she was heading back home to Dominick.

41

Dominick couldn't thank everyone enough or express how much the support from the Spirit of Christmas, still glowing inside of him, meant. When he'd sent up the alarm at Tiffany's disappearance, the whole place had descended into chaos for exactly one minute before everyone snapped into action. Mrs. Claus had never gone missing before, leaving her phone behind. But, even after Dominick explained what had happened, they all agreed there was no way Tiffany could have ascended in a panic, without saying goodbye to anyone. A Claus was always given a chance to explain and say goodbye.

Harvey and Shauna were doing all they could to help Dominick get a hold of Gabriel, but that angel had blocked all their numbers. They also checked every realm they could, even the shithole where Krampus dwelled, and no one had seen her. When he took the time to breathe, Dominick could feel her in his bones, could feel her sadness and confusion. He knew loss and this was something different. His girl was still with him, he just didn't know where.

Dominick did the only logical thing he could. He pulled his shit together and moved forward with the certainty that Tiffany was coming back. He'd found her ring in the sheets and slipped it on his pinky, determined to keep it on him until she was wearing it the proper way again. He continued to send scouts in every direction. He was available to the elves, reindeer and children for anything they were ready to show and teach him as the new Santa Claus.

Every night, for nearly a week, he went to his garage and sat in the prototype sleigh she'd had made for him. He spent hours looking up at the skylights, reassuring himself that what had started between them wasn't over. He dreamt up a million lifetimes they would spend together, the imaginary babies they'd make and how much fun they'd have making them. Mostly though, he thought of her smile and how good it felt to hold her in his arms. No way he was giving up hope that he'd see her again.

On the sixth night, he braced his hands on the edge of the leather driver's seat and let out a loud sigh. He didn't need to sleep, but he knew the idea of Santa's sanity slipping by way of stress insomnia wouldn't boost the already fragile morale of the place. He was about to stand when Pepper and Shadow came trotting through the elephant doors.

"I'm off to bed, ladies, I promise." He stood with a groan and froze when he saw who else had slipped through the door

"Can I join you?" Tiffany said. Dominick stared, praying he wasn't hallucinating. Tiffany crossed the space, looking fresh and renewed. She was wearing the cropped sweatshirt and thigh-hugging sweatpants she had on the first time he'd laid eyes on her. Her silk press had the same wavy bob, but now her hair matched his, a bright silky white.

Dominick slowly stepped out of the sleigh, worried that if he made any sudden moves, she'd disappear. He swallowed and licked his lips. Instead of bursting into tears, he decided humor was the way to go.

"You know, if you're gonna dip out to get milk and chewing tobacco for six days, you should at least take your phone with you. Drop a text or a voice note."

Tiffany stopped in her tracks. "I'm sorry. Did you say six days?"

"Uh, yeah. I may look calm and sexy, but a motherfucker's been stressed. Where'd you go?"

Tiffany rushed over to him and practically leapt into his arms. Dominick hoisted her up, his heart singing when she wrapped her perfect thighs around his waist. "Oh, baby. I'm sorry." She pulled back just enough to look him in the face. "On my end, I was only gone for like twenty minutes."

"Where did you go?"

"Home. Kind of."

Dominick walked them back to the sleigh and took a seat with Tiffany straddling his lap. There was no way he wasn't touching her. She told him the whole story of where she had gone, who she'd been with and the choice she'd been given.

"I know the Lord works in mysterious ways and all that, but I didn't expect that to be so literal. They basically apologized to me for not being clear that you were coming my way."

"You got an apology?"

"Kinda, yeah."

"Talk about being blessed and highly favored."

"They told me not to hold back with you and that you would never hold back with me. So, I need you to know that

I love you, Dominick Bell. I couldn't express how hurt I felt before. I was scared and I didn't feel I had the right to be, but I was so lonely before I met you and it's because you were the love I was waiting for. If you still want me, I think we should spend forever together."

Dominick didn't say anything at first. He just slipped that Asscher-cut diamond off his pinky and slid it right back on her ring finger. "Harvey said it's not tradition here, but I want a wedding. These elves need to know what the deal is."

Tiffany's face lit up. "I'd like that. I've never had a wedding before."

"Well then, I'm your first and I always will be." Dominick leaned in to kiss her, but Tiffany stopped him with a light hand on his chest.

"Um, real quick. I think I might be able to have kids now."

"Say again?"

Tiffany bit her lip and nodded. "Is that something you'd want?"

"With you, yeah, if that's something you'd want. I don't know what magical afterlife pregnancy looks like and it's your body. Or does a Christmas stork just show up with a five-month-old baby that already has a good sense of humor?"

Tiffany snorted. "I think it would mostly be the old fashioned way. But yeah, I do want that with you, in time."

"Let me get one high pressure, twenty-four hour trip around the globe under my belt and then we'll work out the details."

"Deal. I love you."

"I love you, Mrs. Claus."

A brilliant smile spread across Tiffany's face and, for the

first time in almost a week, Dominick felt like he could breathe again. He kissed her long and sweet, every sweep of his lips telling her just how much of a claim she had on his heart.

Eventually, Tiffany pulled back just enough to rest her forehead against his. "We should probably tell Harvey and Shauna I'm back. And, ya know, the rest of the North Pole."

"Yeah, I guess. Harvey's been losing his shit."

"I swear," Tiffany cried. "I thought I was only gone for twenty minutes."

"Yeah, Gabriel's gonna get an email from me." Dominick stood and hoisted Tiffany over his shoulder with ease, smiling as she squealed with glee. They disappeared straight to Harvey's office to give him an in-person proof of life. Then, with firm instructions to spread the news of Mrs. Claus's safe return, they told him they weren't to be disturbed until the morning. They had a lot of reconnecting to do.

42

F*ive years later...*

Tiffany tried to be hands on and present, but sometimes she just had to use her magic to find stuff in her own home. She closed her eyes, picturing the blanket in question, sending out a ping, like sonar. It pinged right back, revealing the blanket's hiding place. She rushed into the great room and found the plush purple fabric shoved between the couch cushions.

"Success!"

Grabbing her phone, blanket in hand, she disappeared back down to the North Pole's flight tower. Dawn was approaching and so were Dominick and his flight crew. So much had changed since their summer wedding all those years ago. She had found herself an amazing, kind, loving husband and the elves had landed themselves a great Santa.

Dominick had learned everything there was to know about running the North Pole and then he started making tweaks, starting with his first decree, that he and Tiffany were equals. He would take the flights, but they would work on everything else together and the elves would come to them both. Tiffany hadn't been sure how the elves would take to such an order, but she'd felt the place change overnight. Tiffany had suddenly felt like she mattered as herself, with all of her experience and know-how, and not just as a facilitator to make Santa's life easier. It was a much-needed change brought on by a man who saw her and loved her. After that, the rest seemed so easy.

Dominick was on his second sleigh, its body taking on the stylish curves of a 1931 Cadillac limousine, after he'd said he wanted to take things old school. On his first flight, he'd hit some bumps along the way. Still, he was one of the best Santas the world had ever seen.

Together, he and the Spirit of Christmas had spread joy, kindness and the love of giving to as many people as they could. On his second turn as a mall Santa, he'd broken up a knife fight in the parking lot and gotten the young boys involved to hug it out and apologize. Last Tiffany had heard, both of them had turned their lives around and one of them was about to start culinary school.

Last year, he'd spotted a lint trap fire while making his rounds and saved a whole family from the blaze. The local news couldn't find the man responsible for the rescue, but the neighbor who had turned over his doorbell cam footage was convinced it was the real Santa. He was doing an amazing job and Tiffany couldn't be prouder.

"How are things looking?" Tiffany asked Jamie, their head of air traffic.

"Good. He'll be approaching soon. Tower to Saint Nick, we have your wife on site."

"Nick to tower. Thank you for the update. Tell her Daddy's on his way and he's got a big present just for her."

"I can hear you, Dom. Stop being nasty."

"Nick to Mrs. Claus. Never."

"I'm sorry, Jamie," Tiffany laughed. "My husband's a pervert."

"It's fine. He's a man in love."

Tiffany scanned the sky and she spotted the sleigh in the distance, Rudolph's glowing nose out in front. "'K, I'm heading down." She rushed to the tarmac, where almost every member of the North Pole was waiting to celebrate another successful trip. She found Chris and Shauna with her special little angel at the front of the crowd.

She gasped with glee when her daughter spotted her from her perch on Uncle Chris's hip. "J.J., look what I found!" Tiffany held up the purple blanket. The kid had access to a world of toys and other furry things, and what she cared about the most was a fleece blanket she'd seen in a Target during her first trip to the human realm. Go figure. Twice a year, Dominick took his girls wherever they wanted to go for a few days and they always ended their trip with one day in L.A. Of course, he couldn't contact anyone from his old life, but Tiffany loved how those trips revived him. It reminded her just how big and beautiful the world was.

J.J. took the blanket and rubbed it all over her chubby cheeks.

"Can you say thank you? Your mommy was looking everywhere for that," Chris said.

"Fank you," J.J. said, her little voice like the sweetest wind chime.

"You're welcome, baby," Tiffany replied.

They'd waited two years. When Waltie's mother had finally passed and called for him to ascend, they'd decided it was time to try for a child of their own. And Dominick had been right about there being a little magic to the whole process. Still, Tiffany had carried their child and would never change a thing about the experience. Jubilee Jefferson Jr. had been named for the two angels who had helped bring her parents together. Tiffany loved her daughter with all her heart and she loved the way Dominick cared for them both. It may have taken a long, long time, but she finally had the family she wanted. She'd forever be grateful for it.

"Here they come!" some elf shouted. All eyes turned to the sky and cheers erupted as Rudolph's shiny nose came into view, the sounds of sleigh bells filling the air. With a graceful ease and perfect teamwork, eight sets of hooves touched down on the runway, bringing the chrome runners to a slow and safe stop. Tiffany couldn't wait. She took off running across the runway, right into Dominick's arms as the elves let out a deafening cheer.

Dominick scooped her up, letting out his booming laugh as she kissed all over his handsome face.

"You're back," she breathed.

"Of course. I had to get home to my girls." His white-gloved hand brushed the hair off her face, then he pressed a deep kiss to her lips. Tiffany felt the weight of a year's worth of preparation lift from her shoulders.

"How did it go?" she asked, as the flight crew came to help Dasher and her team get unhitched and return to the barns for some much needed rest.

"Incident free. I've got a few good stories about some human run-ins, but let me say hi to J.J. before I get into all that."

"Come on." Tiffany took his hand and pulled him through the crowd, as elves offered him pats on the back and congratulations for a job well done. They found Chris and Shauna in the madness.

"Is that my J.J.?" Dominick said over the crowd, before he leveled Chris with a sarcastic smile. "Hand over my kid."

"All this free child care and you still come back with an attitude," Chris teased back as he set Jubilee down. Tiffany's eyes welled with tears of joy as she watched her daughter run into Dominick's arms. He scooped her up, pressing kisses to her sweet face. He'd only been gone for a day, but J.J. had made a mental note of every single thing he'd missed and she was going to tell him about it in painstaking detail as soon as they sat down for their daddy-daughter breakfast.

Dominick turned and held out his hand for Tiffany. She went to him, sliding under his arm, tweaking J.J.'s little toes in her fuzzy boots as they both looked up at him, their hearts full of love and adoration. He declared this Christmas a success, officially starting their winter vacation and all the celebrations to follow.

All day, everyone in the village enjoyed food, music, dancing and laughter. That night, Dominick and Tiffany finally tucked J.J. into her sleigh bed, in the room Shauna had designed for her just off their master suite. Her guardian puppies, Pepper and Shadow, snoozed right on her rug, never far from their princess.

And after their baby was down, Tiffany and her man fell between their own sheets and spent another night worshipping and recommitting themselves to each other.

THE END

ABOUT THE AUTHOR

After years of meddling in her friends' love lives, multi award-winning author Rebekah Weatherspoon turned to writing romance to get her fix. Raised in Southern New Hampshire, Rebekah now lives in Southern California where she will remain forever because she hates moving.

With over twenty-five titles under her belt, Rebekah has covered subgenres including extremely sexy and equally dark romantic suspense, paranormal romance, steamy romantic comedies on horseback, and now young adult romance. With everything going on in the world she still believes in love, the fluffier the better.

You can find praise for Rebekah's books in The New York Times, Entertainment Weekly, Book Riot, Oprah Magazine, TIME Magazine, and on a segment from The Today Show that is definitely pinned at the top of her Instagram page.

To stay up to date on Rebekah's most recent work and events, subscribe to her newsletter at https://rebekahweatherspoon.com/newsletter/

First Edition: December 2024

Credits

Editor: Tara Scott

Cover Art : @chiguma / Instagram and Bluesky

Cover Design: Bree Bridges

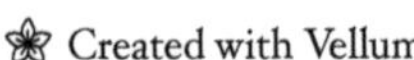
Created with Vellum

www.ingramcontent.com/pod-product-compliance
Ingram Content Group UK Ltd.
Pitfield, Milton Keynes, MK11 3LW, UK
UKHW042003190726
13854UKWH00005B/2150

9 798218 577896